ULTIMATE ENDING

BOOK 5

THE SECRET
OF THE
AURORA HOTEL

Check out the full

ULTIMATE ENDING BOOKS

Series:

TREASURES OF THE FORGOTTEN CITY

THE HOUSE ON HOLLOW HILL

THE SHIP AT THE EDGE OF TIME

ENIGMA AT THE GREENSBORO ZOO

THE SECRET OF THE AURORA HOTEL

THE STRANGE PHYSICS OF THE HEIDELBERG LABORATORY

THE TOWER OF NEVER THERE

*For Colonel Mustard. I always knew it was you, especially once
I found that wrench in the study.*

Welcome to **Ultimate Ending,**
where YOU choose the story!

That's right – everything that happens in this book is a result of decisions YOU make. So choose wisely!

But also be careful. Throughout this book you'll find tricks and traps, trials and tribulations! Most you can avoid with common sense and a logical approach to problem solving. Others will require a little bit of luck. Having a coin handy, or a pair of dice, will make your adventure even more fun. So grab em' if you got em'!

Along the way you'll also find tips, clues, and even items that can help you in your quest. You'll meet people. Pick stuff up. Taking note of these things is often important, so while you're gathering your courage, you might also want to grab yourself a pencil and a sheet of paper.

Keep in mind, there are *many* ways to end the story. Some conclusions are good... some not so good.
Some of them are even great!
But remember:

There is only *ONE*

ULTIMATE
ENDING!

THE SECRET OF THE AURORA HOTEL

Welcome to the Aurora Hotel!

You are SCOTT REINHART, an invited guest on this snowy, blustery Saturday night. An icy wind ushers you up the steps, through the threshold and into the magnificent Grand Lobby.

It's your first time here since your uncle Gus bought the place. Unfortunately you heard it hasn't been doing well. The turn-of-last-century hotel has a long history, and none of it good. You've read reports of freak accidents, of guests disappearing, even tales that the place is haunted! In fact–

"Scotty!"

You trip over your duffel bag as you're nearly tackled to the marble floor. When you look up, it's into the smiling face of your cousin Jenna. Over her shoulder, grinning apologetically, is your other cousin – her twin brother Evan.

"You made it!"

You can't help but laugh. "Of course I made it!" Their email came more than a week ago. Something about them needing help. Something about being able to help your uncle Gus, too. Casually you glance around for him. Except for a few scattered guests, the hotel looks pretty empty.

"Come upstairs," Evan says. "Our rooms are all ready. We can tell you everything."

A half hour later you're all settled in. You and Evan are sharing a room, with Jenna's connected via an adjoining door. Your cousins have been here for a few days, you realize. Since before the snows started to fall. Silently you envy them for missing out on a few days of school.

"So what's this about?" you ask. "Something about... a letter?"

The twins look at each other. Evan reaches into his pocket and pulls out a folded piece of tattered, yellowed paper. The handwriting on it is barely legible.

8

My preparations have been meticulous. The ceremony is arranged.

Alone I have gathered all four artifacts that are somehow still bound to this place. With them I can close the nether-gate -- on this night of all nights -- and restore peace to the Aurora Hotel.

I can only pray that all goes well. That he does not show himself, or interfere in any way.

By tomorrow it will all be over. One way or another.

-- Alastair Roakes   All Hallows Eve, 1909

"Whoa," you say. "Where in the world did you *find* this?"

"In a hidden compartment," Evan replies, "of some antique desk that's bounced its way around the hotel."

"And that's not all," Jenna adds. "There was a photo tucked away with it. An *old* photo."

"Is that him?" you ask. "This... Alastair guy?"

The twins nod in unison. "We guess so," Jenna says. "I mean, that's what we're counting on, anyway."

Counting on? Counting on for what?

[**Remember this page number** to refer back to this photo at any time]

10

Jenna casts her brother a concerned look. "Evan, tell him."

Your cousin looks uncomfortable. Then again, he usually does. Evan's the smartest guy you know, but he was never good with people. Or words. "Things are bad here," he begins. "Something is... well, something is *wrong* with this place."

"What do you mean by wrong?"

He pauses, searching for the right words. "My father is worried, Scott. When he bought this place he got it cheap, so he knew something was probably up. But he always thought it was something he could fix. Some new plaster here, some fresh paint there – that sort of thing. Hey, the place is old. It's expected. Only the longer we stay here, the weirder it gets."

"Not weird, haunted!" Jenna cries. You can tell your more vociferous cousin was a having a hard time keeping silent. "This place is creepy, cuz. People have seen things. *We've* seen things. It's driving the customers away and making things miserable for dad."

You blink. So that's why the hotel seems practically empty. But *haunted?* For some reason it doesn't make sense. For Jenna to be convinced, maybe, but Evan has always been the more rational of the two.

"So what can *I* do?" you ask. "Why'd you call me up here?"

Evan holds up the letter. "Four artifacts," he reads. He points to the photograph. "Now look on the table. A bell, a candle, a crystal ball–"

"–and a book," Jenna adds. "Don't forget about the book."

You study the photo. The man seated at the table certainly *appears* like he's about to conduct some sort of ceremony. The four strange artifacts lay spread out before him. *An arrangement,* you think quietly.

"Let's say this is Alastair," you offer. "So what? This guy is long gone. The ceremony is long since over."

"Not if he never finished it," Jenna says. Her eyes sparkle with a contagious excitement. "Think about it, Scotty. This guy Alastair knew the hotel was haunted. His ceremony was meant to put it at rest. Only it's *not* at rest, which means whatever he was trying to do didn't work. He failed, or–"

"–or he got interrupted," Evan finishes. "See what it says? Hopefully 'he' won't show himself. So who is 'he'? And what if he *did* show himself?"

Evan pauses. "A long time ago, there was a big explosion here, in the basement of the hotel. We looked it up. Know when it was?"

"1909?"

"Yes. Halloween night. Or all Hallows' Eve, depending on how you phrase it." Your cousin's eyes narrow. You've never seen him this focused. "We're thinking this 'he' showed up. Messed up Alastair's plans."

"There's a pile of guest logs in the old storage room," Jenna goes on. "The records say an Alastair Roakes checked into the Aurora a few days before the explosion. But he never paid his bill. He never checked out."

You let loose a broken chuckle. "Think he's still here?" When you look up though, your cousins aren't laughing.

"This *'he'* guy might still be here," Evan shrugs. "Might even be the bad guy people keep seeing around. Maybe he's the one responsible for this 'nethergate' in the first place."

Bad guy? You decide not to ask. "So what's the plan?"

"Simple," Jenna says. "We search the Aurora top to bottom for these four objects. When we've gathered them all, maybe we can somehow finish the ceremony."

"And close the nethergate," Evan adds. "Solve the whole ghost problem here, once and for all."

You nod. Seems simple enough. Too simple, actually. "The bell, candle, crystal and book... wouldn't these things be long gone by now?"

"Not if they were *bound* to this place," Evan answers. "Like it says here in the letter."

A smile crosses your face, mirroring Jenna's. "Sure, why not? I'm in!" Your cousins' enthusiasm is rubbing off on you. "But how are we going to search this place while guests are here? Won't uncle Gus – I mean your dad – come down on us?"

"That's why we wait until midnight," Jenna says. "Most of the hotel will be shut down. We'll have free run of the place!"

"Plus," Evan adds, "after midnight the date will be right too. It'll be All Hallows' Eve..."

12

A few hours and a couple of cheeseburgers later (courtesy of Uncle Gus!) you're still relaxing in your room. Despite everyone agreeing to try to get some rest, you're just too excited to sleep tonight. Still, your eyes are getting heavy when suddenly–

"Happy Halloween!" Jenna bursts through your suite door like a kid on Christmas morning. It's not even two seconds after midnight. "You guys ready?"

"Yeah..." Evan groans as he sits up. "In a few."

As Jenna bounces over you notice she's holding something. "What's that?"

"I swiped the master key from the front desk," she declares proudly. Your cousin shakes a piece of paper in her other hand. "And the guest manifest, too. That way we can tell which rooms are empty."

"Nice!" You squint curiously at the large bronze key Jenna is spinning around the tip of her finger. "Wow, they still use *keys* here?"

"It's an old hotel," Evan explains. "It's all part of the charm."

Jenna chuckles. "You sound like dad, trying to save money." She flops onto the bed. "Okay, we only have until morning. 42 rooms, three floors... this place is big. Evan and I already decided we're gonna need to split up."

Evan swipes the key mid-spin, then takes a copy of the manifest from his sister. "I'll take this level. The first floor. See what I can find."

"And I'll start at the lobby level," Jenna says. "There's lots of stuff to check out downstairs."

"Once we're done, we can meet up at the elevator," Evan says. "Then we can all do the second floor together. Cool?"

"Cool!" cries Jenna. She whirls to face you. "So Scotty... the big question: Who you goin' with?"

Time to decide!

If you'd like to search the lobby level of the hotel with Jenna, *TURN TO PAGE 63*

If you'd rather check out the first floor of the Aurora with Evan, *HEAD OVER TO PAGE 94*

Ghost-voice or not, you're not ready to surrender. So you keep fighting, keep shoving back with all your might. Your invisible assailant covers you like a blanket, crushing you to the hard oak floor.

The pressure is crippling. It's getting harder to breathe. You suck one last breath into your deflated lungs, and use it to shout – and to push back – as loudly and defiantly as possible!

Quick, roll two dice! (Or just pick a random number from 2 to 12)
If the total of your roll is a 9 or higher, *GO TO PAGE 27*
If the total of your roll is an 8 or lower, *TURN TO PAGE 118*

14

Back out in the hallway, your cousin consults the manifest. "I think we're pretty much done with–"

The *ding* of the elevator splits the silence. It's hard to imagine who it might be at this hour. You and Evan crouch down, ready for anything, when the doors slide open. But the elevator is empty.

"That's strange," Evan says. "It's not like–"

"YAAHHH!"

Jenna springs from one side of the elevator, roaring like a lion! Your heart skips three beats. Evan jumps a foot into the air and comes down clutching his chest.

"Hey bro! Hey cuz!" It takes Jenna a moment to stop laughing. "Wow, I wish I'd filmed that. If only you could've seen your faces!"

Evan is thoroughly unamused. "Quit clowning around," he hisses. "People are sleeping! If anyone wakes up, or calls in a complaint to the front desk–"

"Relax," Jenna assures him. She pulls you both into the elevator and allows the doors to close. You notice she's chewing on a very large cookie. "Snagged it from the kitchen," she says in answer to your inquiring look. "So hey, did you guys find anything?"

"Actually yes," her brother announces proudly. "While you were down there having snack time we managed to find the crystal ball *and* the bell."

Jenna's eyes light up. "That's great!" Reaching behind her she pulls forth a large rectangular object. "I found Alastair's book in the library." As she pauses you examine the tome. There's no mistaking it. It looks exactly like the book from the photograph. "But this," she says, fishing a small yellowed candle from her pocket, "was a *lot* harder to get a hold of."

"Nice!" you grin. Your cousin beams back at you before sticking her tongue out at her brother. "So we have everything right? All four artifacts?"

"Yup!" Jenna answers. "Everything we need to recreate that broken, hundred year-old ceremony."

A blast of cold air suddenly chills you to the bone. Which is extremely odd, considering you're all standing in a closed elevator.

"*Not exactly...*" rasps a voice that doesn't belong to any of you.

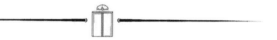

Uh oh.

Better hurry up and *TURN TO PAGE 146*

"We need to get out of here," you say with a rising sense of urgency. "Stay here while l try the left door."

Your cousins appear very uneasy about your choice. Before they can protest (or your bravery dissolves away) you pull open the left-side door and step through.

The floor is white. The walls... *are there even walls anymore?* You're suddenly not so sure. You continue walking, searching for anything recognizable. Eventually, way off in the distance, you see a pair of dark objects. With nothing else to do, you walk toward them.

The journey takes forever. Step after step, it feels like you're walking for miles. Panic grips you. You're about to start running, for fear of being trapped here, when all of sudden you're standing behind two people.

It's Jenna and Evan! You tap your female cousin on her shoulder.

"Jeeze!" Jenna cries, jumping forward about three feet. "Don't scare me like that!"

"Sorry," you apologize. "I just–"

Evan looks absolutely dumbstruck. He glances from you, to the door, then back to you again. "Wait. How did you... get..." He rubs his eyes in disbelief.

"That place is forever," you say, although you realize the statement probably makes little sense. "Thanks for waiting for me though."

Jenna stares back at you in confusion. "Scotty, you *just* walked through the door," she says. "Literally ten seconds ago."

A shiver runs through you from head to toe. "Well then that's definitely the wrong exit," you breathe.

No harm no foul, right? Choose again!

If you want to try the door on the right, *HEAD TO PAGE 30*
If you'd rather try the window instead, *TURN TO PAGE 122*

16

"Let's check out the office," you suggest, "before she comes back." Jenna agrees, and together you enter the brightly-lit room behind the front desk.

The manager's office is neat, orderly. Exactly what you'd expect from your uncle Gus. However, there doesn't seem to be much to search through. Heck, you're not exactly sure what you're looking for to begin with.

"There, the back room," Jenna points to a small wooden door. It's so narrow and tucked away you never would've noticed it. "The older stuff is kept back there."

A metal desk blocks your way. It's easily moved, but the grinding sound it makes as you slide it to one side sends a shiver up the back of your neck... like nails on a chalkboard. Once inside, you realize there's no light. Not even a light switch. Dust covers everything. The room has a woody, old book smell to it. Like the deepest part of a library.

Your cousin pulls out her cell phone. Using it as a flashlight she being rifling through a ream of old papers. "I saw something here once," she says, "back when Evan and I were looking through the old hotel manifests. There were a couple of black and white photographs. They showed some of the – ah, here they are..."

She's holding three tattered photos. They all depict the same thing; an old, Victorian-style house taken from three different angles. In the third photo, a man stands off to one side. His features are blurred, like he moved or something during the process of having his picture taken.

"Who's this guy?" you ask. The photo is more than a little intriguing.

"Oh, I don't know. But here, this is what I wanted to show you." With one finger, Jenna traces an old wall of stacked stones. "See that? That wall is still here. It's just outside, along the east side of the Aurora."

You nod, having noticed the wall yourself when you first came in. It didn't seem to fit with the hotel at all. "So that would put this guy's house right... here. Exactly where we're standing."

Jenna nods. "Think maybe he's mad this hotel got built right over his home?" she asks. You glance back at the third photo and your blood runs cold. The blurred man is miraculously sharp now, totally crisp. He's hunched over slightly, staring back at you with unmistakable anger. No, something much more powerful than anger. Hate.

"Yeah," you say shakily. "I'm sure of it."

Time to go before Agnes comes back.

If you want to check out the fireplace, *FLIP DOWN TO PAGE 77*

Or if you'd rather see the taxidermy room, *GO TO PAGE 112*

18

"Stick to the shadows," you tell Jenna. "Don't step into the moonlight."

Your cousin shrugs but obeys. She starts by gingerly stepping into the first dark square. When nothing happens she continues on, moving gracefully from one to the other. By the end she's even playing hopscotch with herself. But on the very last square...

CLICK!

Part of the ceiling above Jenna slides to one side. A ramp drops out, falling to land right beside her. On its ancient surface, worn wooden steps lead upward into darkness.

"Whoa," your cousin swears. She runs a hand over the bottom step. "What's this?"

"An invitation," you say. The ramp looks thick, sturdy. It could easily support your combined weight. "But do we take it?"

You and Evan follow the shadow squares to stand beside Jenna, where your cousin uses his cell phone flashlight to penetrate the darkness. "There's a room up there," he says. "Which is nuts, because we're already on the top level."

You place a foot on the first step. "Ready?"

Surprisingly, both of your cousins nod enthusiastically. "Let's get to the bottom, err – I mean top of this," Evan says.

Climb the steps and enter the darkness when you *TURN TO PAGE 142*

Jenna leaps up, ushering you forward. There's no time to argue. Her hand is pressed urgently into your back.

"This way!" she says. For the first time tonight there's fear in her voice. You don't like it all. "We have to–"

CLANG!

It all happens so fast – there's no time to react. Jenna clips a handle on one of the pots of boiling water. It tips... falls... lands right beside you! Scalding hot water sloshes out, splattering across your cousin's leg...

"OWWW!!"

Jenna falls, clutching her shin. A half-second later you're beside her, squeezing her hand, trying to comfort her as she twists in pain. Marco shows up. He looks terrified. He shouts for someone else, and then Uncle Gus is there, his face drawn with worry.

"Call an ambulance!" your Uncle shouts. You pull out your phone and immediately dial the emergency number. When you look back at Jenna, her expression is a mixture of agony and apology.

The kitchen? Really? You should've been more careful. But you weren't, which makes this

THE END

20

It's the urgency of Evan's voice that changes your mind. With a final look over your shoulder, you climb back through the window.

"Good," he says. "Glad you're not *totally* crazy."

You let out a laugh. "Like your sister?"

"Exactly." Evan slides the window closed. Almost instantly, the world beyond it goes dark.

'Whoa."

The two of you watch as it happens again. The sun shoots up in a matter of seconds, but it also goes dark just as fast. With each 'day' that blinks by, the landscape changes. It goes from desert to grasslands. It's a swamp. A mountainside. An ocean. A sheet of ice. At one point you see a jagged tower silhouetted against the distant horizon, all dark and strange. Then, just as quickly, it's gone. Everything happens in under a minute. A cold shiver runs through your body.

"Thanks," you breathe. "For not letting me go out there."

Evan nods numbly. Then together you turn and race each other back to the hallway.

Rock-solid choice back there.

Now *HEAD OVER TO PAGE 108*

"I don't like that sound," you say with growing concern. "Let's go this way!"

You grab Jenna's hand and sprint down the left-hand corridor. Almost immediately you smash into something big and solid... and get knocked to the floor. You look up into the very confused and then angry face of your Uncle Gus!

"What in the world are you two doing down here!" he cries. Your uncle glances down at his watch. "Do you have any *idea* what time it is?"

"I– Yes, well... we–"

"Get upstairs and back in your rooms!" your uncle says sternly. You watch as he shoots his daughter a look of suspicion. "In fact, let's go. I'm walking you there myself so you don't take any detours."

Jenna's shoulders slump. She shrugs at you helplessly as you're led back to your rooms with specific orders not to leave for the rest of the night. "And believe me," Uncle Gus says to punctuate his instructions, "I'll be checking."

Well, it looks like your adventure ended before it really got started. But hey, at least the ghosts won't get you tonight. You hope...

Unfortunately however, this looks like

THE END

22

"I'm gonna try the red door," you announce.

"Why that one?"

"Why not?" you shoot back. Sometimes Evan can be *too* analytical. You reach and close your hand over the knob...

ZAP!

A huge jolt of electricity explodes outward, arcing from the knob to your hand. It travels along the length of your arm and into your shoulder, causing your body to seize involuntarily. Luckily this makes you fall backward, away from the door.

"*That's* why not," Evan smirks once he realizes you're okay. "Bro, we need to be more careful."

"Amen to that," you say, rubbing your hand.

Pick again! And this time try not to hurt yourself!

If you choose the *BLUE* door, *FLIP TO PAGE 106*

If you choose the *GREEN* door, *FLIP TO PAGE 136*

If you choose the *BLACK* door, *FLIP TO PAGE 36*

If you choose the *GOLD* door, *FLIP TO PAGE 145*

Jenna waits until Vincent's attention is focused once again on cleaning the rug. Then she noses over to the janitor's open closet. "Let's check it out."

"Really?"

"Yeah really," your cousin says. "Don't you want to be thorough? Besides, it's not like we're gonna *steal* anything."

The two of you slip inside. The janitor's closet is, as you might expect, packed with cleaning supplies. You squeeze past mops and sponges, brooms and dustpans. A large aluminum stepladder leans against one wall. The entire place smells overwhelmingly of ammonia and bleach.

"None of that stuff will be in here," you say. "Vincent already said–"

"Hey, wait. What's a cupola?"

Jenna is staring at a labeled pegboard of tools and trinkets. At the very end is a strange, square-shaped key marked with the word 'Cupola" above it.

"It's that turret on the roof of the hotel," you tell her. Your cousin still looks confused. "The little spike-shaped building with all the windows. I noticed it from the road."

"Oh, *that* thing!" Jenna exclaims. "I've always wanted to go up there!" Before you can say anything she unhooks the tiny square key and slips it into her pocket.

"Uh, I thought we weren't going to steal anything," you point out.

Jenna grins. "Who's stealing? We're just gonna *borrow* this for a little while."

Slip out of the janitor's office and head to the hotel lounge by *TURNING TO PAGE 49*

24

The three of you enter room 212. Right away, you're taken aback by the unmistakable sounds of crying.

Sitting on the bed is the ghostly image of a woman dressed in dated clothing. Her face rests in her hands. She's sobbing softly.

"Wh-what's wrong with her?" Jenna asks, her voice cracking. You notice your cousin's eyes are glazed over. It makes sense. Since stepping foot into the room, you yourself are overcome with an almost paralyzing sense of sorrow.

Evan however, is staring off into space. His attention is lost, as if in a trance or under some kind of spell. You call out to him several times. There's no reaction.

"Can we help you?" you ask the woman. You rub your own eyes and find them filled with tears. "Is there something–"

"*She's trapped,*" Evan says, in a voice not his own. It sounds mechanical. Almost robotic.

"What do you mean she's trapped?" Jenna asks. She shoots her brother a look of legitimate concern.

"*She lost something,*" Evan continues, "*long ago. She cannot leave until she is given something of beauty.*"

"Something of beauty?" you repeat. You look at yourself, at Evan, and Jenna. Do any of you even have something like that?

212

If you have something of beauty, what is it? Add up the letters in that word using the chart below, and *TURN TO THAT PAGE*

A = 1	F = 6	K = 11	P = 16	U = 21	Z = 26
B = 2	G = 7	L = 12	Q = 17	V = 22	Example:
C = 3	H = 8	M = 13	R = 18	W = 23	ANNA =
D = 4	I = 9	N = 14	S = 19	X = 24	1+14+14+1
E = 5	J = 10	O = 15	T = 20	Y = 25	= 30

If you don't have anything to give the woman, *HEAD TO PAGE 111*

26

"If anyone has that key," Jenna says, "it's Vincent, the janitor." Before you or Evan can say anything else she pushes the lobby button. "So let's go find out."

The elevator rumbles to a stop and the three of you pad quietly through the lobby. Agnes the night receptionist is motionless at the front desk. She might even be sleeping.

"There," Jenna indicates. She points to an open closet just off the wide main hallway, where a man is in the process of putting away a large floor-cleaning machine. "He's finishing up for the night."

You watch as Vincent shuffles out of the maintenance closet. He disappears around the next corner while rolling up a long extension cord.

"Now's our chance," Evan urges. "He hangs the key ring in the closet every night before locking up. Let's swipe it."

"Unless," Jenna says, "he hasn't hung it up yet. Listen, Vincent likes me. Let me go talk to him."

"What?"

"He's cool," Jenna explains. "He'd give me the key if I asked for it." She cracks her gum. "Trust me."

Your gaze shifts back and forth as you watch your cousins argue. Jenna's eyes are pleading. Evan is shaking his head back and forth in a 'no way' gesture.

They both turn toward you expectantly. It's obvious you'll need to settle this.

Do you trust Jenna that Vincent will be cool? If so, send her to talk to the janitor *BY TURNING TO PAGE 80*

Of course, Jenna thinks everyone's cool. If it's too risky, try to swipe the janitor's key ring *OVER ON PAGE 116*

You open your throat and let loose a scream so loud it hurts you own ears! And in the background, more dimly, you can hear Evan screaming too.

But it's no use. As the last of your oxygen leaves your lungs, you feel light-headed. Dizzy. The intense pressure is still there, like a weight, crushing you. Only you can no longer fight it. No longer struggle against the blackness as it works its way in from the corners of your vision...

"Scott! SCOTT!"

You blink awake. Uncle Gus is leaning over you, his face whiter than the sheets of the bed you've been laid out on. He looks absolutely terrified.

"Scott!" Another voice. Jenna, seated beside you. A wave of relief floods over your uncle as you begin moving your lips again.

"Wh-what happened?"

"We found you here in room 105, lying unconscious – the both of you!" Uncle Gus says. Your cousin Evan moves into view now, looking pale and haggard. "A guest reported hearing you screaming," he continues. "What were you even *doing* in here?"

It's a fair question, and one you don't have a very easy answer for. Thankfully, whatever gripped you must have finally let go. You're going to be okay.

As for your quest to help the Aurora however, it looks like this is

THE END

28

"You're probably right," you tell your cousin. "You're light enough to climb these things without breaking them, so you should search the shelves at the top. I'll do the lower rows."

Jenna flashes you her fiercest grin. Three seconds later she's at the top of a bookshelf, her hands moving furiously. The almost hypnotic *thump thump thump* of books being slammed on their spines is the only sound in the room.

You get to work. At first it's slow going, but you soon find yourself falling into a steady rhythm. Your mind wanders to the hotel, the hauntings... all the problems your cousins have written you about. You only hope you can help them – and your uncle Gus – fix whatever is wrong here.

"Halfway done and still nothing," Jenna calls down from one of the stacks. The two of you continue for several more minutes, turning the orderly bookshelves into a chaotic jumble of mismatched tomes. Down to the last few shelves, you start to lose faith. When suddenly...

"GOT IT!"

You look up to find Jenna beaming, waving a dust-covered book with thick brass corner-guards. She shimmies down from the top of a stack, and together you compare it to the book in the photo. "It's a perfect match," you agree. "Nice job!"

"Thanks cuz!" Her eyes shift in a circle around the large room. "Wow, we'd better go. We already spent too much time here."

You pause at the exit, casting one last glance back into the hotel library. It looks like a tornado hit the place. "Um, what about the mess? Won't Uncle Gu– I mean your father, be mad?"

"Nah," Jenna says, blowing a bubble the size of her face. You resist the urge to pop it. "It's Halloween, remember? We'll just blame the ghosts!"

Great job! You found the book!

Proceed into the hotel's Regency Ballroom when you *FLIP TO PAGE 139*

You yank back on the vent cover. *Hard.*

The grating pops free!   Only it happens a lot easier than you thought it would.   There's a split second of regret as you tumble backward, and that's when you feel a sharp stinging across your arm.

"Scott!" Evan exclaims, rushing forward. "Are you alright?"

You think so... that is, until you look down at your forearm. There's a nasty gash there from wrist to elbow! Your eyes go to the razor sharp edges of the vent cover. Maybe you should've thought this through...

"Oh man, you're bleeding bad," Evan says. He rushes into the bathroom and comes back with a towel. Of course the towel is red. "You're going to need stitches. A lot of them!"

There's blood on the floor, the rug, the wall. "Hey, at least I'm not staining anything," you smile weakly. But there's no humor in it. Not now. I mean, what are you going to tell your Uncle Gus? That you just *happened* to tear your whole arm open at one o'clock in the morning? Your stomach sinks just thinking about it.

Your trip to the emergency room is just beginning. But your quest to help the Aurora hotel is unfortunately at

THE END

30

The constant vertigo of this room is making you sick. With no time to waste, you pick the right-hand door.

It opens into light. Or maybe darkness. As odd as it sounds, it's impossible to know what's on the other side unless you step through. You do it without thinking... as if drawn through the doorway by some unseen force.

"Jenna, Evan, I'll be right–"

You look behind you. Of course the door is gone. Everything's gone, really, including you. Because no matter where you look, or how you turn, a landscape of nothingness stretches in all directions.

Limbo sure looks boring, but at least you'll have a long time to explore it. As far as solving the mysteries of the Aurora Hotel however, this is definitely

THE END

Fumbling in your pocket, you pull out the odd stone cube you and Evan had found earlier. You rotate it until the writing is on the correct side, and then slide it into the ledge.

The cube fits the hole perfectly! For a few seconds nothing happens, but then you hear the loud grinding of stone on stone.

"Look!" Jenna points.

Directly above you, a stone ladder now leads straight up to the roof! The depressions have inverted themselves, creating perfect hand and footholds with which to climb.

Evan's face is painted with tremendous relief. He even smiles.

"Go go go!" you tell him, sending him up after Jenna. A brief, simple climb later, and all three of you are at the edge of the Aurora's vast rooftop.

Pretty cool!

See what happens next *OVER ON PAGE 104*

32

You stand with your hands out, fingers splayed in your best non-threatening gesture.

"Sir, please listen to us. We entered your room by accident. We never–"

"Liar!" the man shouts. "See? You even have a key!" He nods at Evan, who happens to be still holding the Aurora's skeleton key.

Jenna gazes wistfully over at the fire escape. More and more it's looking like a good idea.

The man's face dawns with sudden recognition. "Hang on a second," he says. "I know you. You're the owner's kids. The twins, right?"

Evan's shoulders drop. "Yes," he admits. "But we–"

"Don't say anything else!" the man sneers. "I'm calling the front desk." He grabs the phone from one of the nightstands. "Let's see what security has to say about this whole thing..."

Your stomach drops. Explaining this to your Uncle Gus is going to be quite difficult. And since he'll be here soon, we might as well call this

---

THE END

You don't wait. You don't ask. Poking two fingers through the ancient wallpaper, you tear a slit all the way down to the floor. It's just large enough to crawl through.

"Scott!" Evan calls from behind you. "Wait!"

The area behind the wallpaper is a world of darkness. Carefully you stand up without hitting your head on anything. Dust fills your nostrils. The air smells stale. Your fingers tremble as you fish out your cell phone and thumb the flashlight.

You're in a long closet, or maybe a small room. There's barely enough space to move around, which makes it even more crowded when Evan suddenly appears next to you.

"Curiosity finally got you, didn't it?"

"Yeah, sure," he replies. "That, plus I'm not too thrilled with the idea of explaining to my father how you got swallowed by a wall."

Your phone still paints the room with light. There's nothing much in here at all. A row of shelves line the far wall, empty but for a single, square-shaped item. Evan grabs it.

"It's a stone cube," your cousin tells you. He turns it over a few times in his palm before handing it over. "There's some kind of writing on one side. Symbols, maybe."

You shrug and place the cube in your pocket. It feels heavy against your leg.

"Let's get out of here," you tell your cousin. "Before that ghost comes back."

Backtrack into the hallway when you *TURN TO PAGE 108*

34

The more you think about climbing that ladder, the more you hate the whole idea. "Let's try slinging those candles down," you tell Jenna.

Your cousin wastes no time. She twirls her homemade sling in a wide circle, using smooth movements that make you wonder if she's somehow done this before. Her first cast falls short of the chandelier. Her second one sails past it. The third throw is wild; and strikes the side of the antique fixture with a clang. The candelabra sways back and forth as the dust of decades rains down on you.

"Easy!"

"I'm trying to be," Jenna says. "I'm just being careful not to get it stuck."

It turns out the fourth time's the charm. The string goes the center of the fixture and you catch the counterweight on the way down. Each of you pull on one end of the string, stripping most of the candles from their holders.

With growing alarm you realize you hadn't thought about this part at all! A half dozen of them drop toward the floor...

"*That* one!" Jenna cries. "The one with the triangle on it!"

Quick! How fast are you? Roll a single die:

If you rolled a 2 or a 4, *TURN TO PAGE 120*

If you rolled a 1, 3, 5 or 6, *FLIP OVER TO PAGE 85*

The lock sticks to the next room, which is 112. Evan fumbles with the key for a minute before you finally hear the *click*.

The door opens into a maelstrom of dust. It covers the floor, the furniture, and every last surface of the room. You find yourself leaving footprints as you walk the oaken floor. Obviously the hotel hasn't rented this place in years.

"We rent this place all the time," Evan says, as if reading your mind. "But there's something about this room. No matter how much we clean it, it always gets like this."

All of a sudden something hits you in the face! Your arms go up instinctively, hands frantically swatting the air as you brush away the remnants of a giant spiderweb.

"This might be a good place to look," Evan says, ignoring your plight. "Let's get on it."

You check dresser drawers, night tables, the armoire – everything comes up empty. Your cousin eventually emerges from the bathroom, shrugging. You're about to go when you hear him gasp with a sharp intake of breath.

"What is it?"

Evan only points. You follow his arm down to the floor, where a message is scrawled in the thick layer of dust:

I will NEVER leave!

"That definitely wasn't there when we first came in," you say unnecessarily. Evan nods in mute agreement. You stand there wondering, hand resting on one of the posts of the four-poster bed, when you notice something scratchy against your palm. Something that contrasts with the smoothness of the wood.

"Umm..." You remove your hand and motion your cousin over. There's a word there, carved crudely into the post: *WARRICK*.

"Who's Warrick?" you ask.

Evan shakes his head back and forth slowly. "Good question." He opens his mouth weirdly for a moment, but it's only to let out a violent sneeze. "Come on," he sniffs. "Let's go."

112

Better get out of here before you start sneezing too. *TURN TO PAGE 126*

36

You step up to the black door. You're not even sure why. Reaching out, you turn the knob and pull...

The door doesn't open. But instantly, a haunting laughter resonates from all around you. It's a loud, taunting, horrible laughter that should be terrifying... but it's not. Instead, for some strange reason, it makes you feel overwhelmingly sad.

You try to take your hand from the knob, but you can't. You have no more control over your arm than you would over Evan's. You can only stand there weeping, tears running down both cheeks as your soul fills with melancholy. As the laughter continues, the melancholy is followed by an incredible sense of dread. It rises up in your chest, filling your lungs. Choking you...

Hurry! Flip a coin!

If it comes up *HEADS* you should *TURN TO PAGE 84*

If it comes up *TAILS* you ought to *HEAD TO PAGE 52*

You look the glass elevator up and down. "I've always wanted to ride one of these," you tell Jenna. "Let's go."

Stepping into the old elevator is like stepping through time. Ten long panes of glass are arranged in a circular pattern, chased by gold leaf accents and polished wood paneling. The elevator dips significantly as you step into it. As Jenna jumps in after you, your stomach lurches.

"Where are the buttons?"

Your cousin laughs. "No buttons, silly." For the first time you notice a pair of long metal handles that sprout from the floor. Jenna grabs one and pulls it toward her, causing the elevator to lurch uncomfortably.

"On second thought, maybe we should take the–"

The elevator drops a few inches, jolting you right out of your sentence. Then it starts descending. You look out through windows, into the sprawling, well-lit hotel lobby. But just as you're getting comfortable...

"This thing..." Jenna says. She now appears to be wrestling with the controls. "It's always getting stuck. I don't know why–"

You drop. It happens so suddenly your mind doesn't even have time to register what's going on. One second you're enjoying the view, the next your stomach is somewhere up near your Adam's apple. As the elevator crashes toward the floor of the lobby, Jenna pulls back on the other stick with all her might.

Screeeeeeeeeecch!

The car shudders to a stop only a few inches above the floor. You hear a musical *clink clink clink* as one of the long glass panes becomes spider-webbed with jagged cracks.

"Oh man, Dad's not gonna like that one," Jenna quips. She doesn't seem the least bit phased by what you've already chalked up as a near-death experience. "Come on," she says. "Let's investigate the lobby."

Check out the lobby by *FLIPPING TO PAGE 68*

38

Evan pauses before the next door. It looks just like every other door in the hallway, only the number plate is missing. Numerically, it falls between rooms 113 and 115. But since the even numbered rooms are on the other side of the hallway, that makes no sense at all.

"Maybe we should skip this room," your cousin says. There's an edge of nervousness to his voice. "I've never been in here."

You take the key from his hand. "No," you say, unlocking the door. "That's exactly why we *shouldn't* skip it."

Inside, the room is disappointingly plain. You and Evan get to work, and it doesn't take long to complete a thorough search. You're about to declare the room empty when you notice your cousin hasn't moved in a while. He's standing at one of the three windows, a look of confusion drawn upon his face.

"Come look at this," he tells you. You follow his gaze. Not far from the hotel the landscape is blanketed by a thick forest of very large trees.

"Is that the rear grounds?" you ask. "Not very developed for such an old hotel, no? But hey, at least it stopped snowing."

"That's just it," Evan says. "This window is in the front. We should be looking out over the parking lot right now." His voice cracks. "And the snow didn't stop – it's just gone. We had at least two feet of accumulation when you got here. And now... nothing."

He's right. Curiously you move to the next window, where the landscape gets even weirder. Still no snow, but now moonlight glints off a lake, or maybe even an ocean. You could swear you see waves off in the distance, relentlessly pounding the shore.

"How could this be?"

But Evan is already looking through the third window, set perpendicularly into another wall. Beyond it the landscape is barren, totally devoid of anything. *Like a desert*, you think.

"That's impossible," Evan says, rapping against the glass. "This last window can't even be here. This isn't a corner room."

Almost in answer the window glides silently open. Evan jumps back, his whole body covered in gooseflesh.

You step past him and lean outside. The air beyond the window feels totally different. Down below, what looks like sand is piled up against the side of Aurora's facade.

"This ledge looks wide enough to stand on," you say, placing your hands on it. "Maybe we could step out and get a better look."

When you duck back inside your cousin looks absolutely horrified.

Want to step out onto the ledge and see what's up? *TURN TO PAGE 76*

Or maybe Evan's right and you should skip this room. If so, *GO TO PAGE 108*

40

Elephant tusk... elephant tusk... you know you've seen one before, but where?

"The blue room!" you exclaim. "There was an elephant tusk in the blue room!"

Both of your cousins are looking at you funny.

Hurry up and *TURN TO PAGE 119*

After a quick breather, Evan unlocks the door to room 108. You step inside, only to be surrounded – no, buried – by references to the 1970's.

The level of detail is impressive. Every piece of furniture screams retro, from the white shag carpet that covers the floor to the giant spinning disco ball that dangles from the ceiling. In the center of the room, a perfectly round bed is made up with zebra skin linens.

"Wow," you say. "Is there a 1980's room too?"

"Yes," Evan says, "but that one's always rented out."

You laugh. "Why? Does it come with a Hot Tub Time Machine?"

"I wish," Evan replies. "If it did, we could just go back to 1909 and stop Alastair from performing the ceremony."

"Oh, I can think of a lot of other places I'd go first," you quip.

The rest of the room looks complicated, with many places to check. An open door leads into a bathroom on your right.

"Okay," Evan says. "Pick your poison. You want to do in here, or in there?"

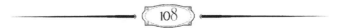

108

If you want to search the bedroom, *TURN TO PAGE 160*
If you'd rather search the bathroom, *HEAD TO PAGE 54*

42

The air gets cooler as the elevator rumbles past the basement. Then, abruptly, it comes to a shuddering stop. The doors open.

"This isn't the hotel anymore," Evan says. "Look at the floor..."

You step out of the elevator, the three of you converting your cell phones into flashlights. The floor is hard-packed dirt, mixed with cobbles worn smooth by time. The walls are equally rough, and also dirt in some places.

"Is this the sub-basement?" you ask.

"Sort of," Jenna says. "All this was definitely here before the Aurora was constructed. Looks like they built the new basement over it, but someone still gave the elevator access."

Cobwebs dangle everywhere. You walk with your arm out in front of you to brush them away. Broken brick walls stand partially collapsed on both sides, giving way to a curved passage up ahead. You continue along until the passage opens into a larger area.

Jenna gasps. "Look!"

The chamber before you is squared off. It has the details of an actual room rather than a cave. It's also completely blackened. The floor is singed, the walls charred as if from–

"The explosion!" Jenna says. "It happened here!" She pulls out the photograph and points to two spots along the back wall. "Look, you can see where the bookshelves once stood. The walls are lighter there."

"And that's not all," Evan calls from a corner of the room. Leaning against the wall is a round, oaken table. You rush over and help your cousin pull it into a standing position. Each of you take a side, while Jenna uses the photograph to help guide it into position.

"Hang the lamp Scotty," Jenna tells you. "You're the tall one."

You glance up at the ceiling. There's a hook there, exactly where you'd expect it to be. Your cousins arrange the other artifacts on the table as you hang the lamp from its chain. When you finally step back, everything looks pretty much as it does in the photograph.

"What now?" Jenna asks.

Evan pulls an an elaborate, high-backed chair from the shadows. He places it behind the table. "This."

Your cousin stares down at the chair. "I guess I'll do the honors," he sighs. But as he goes to sit down, you stop him.

"Let me do it."

Evan looks at you funny. "Why?"

"Honestly?" you shrug. "I don't even know." The truth is, you really don't. "But you guys asked me out here to help, so let me help."

"And what if something goes wrong?" Evan counters.

You laugh. It's a nervous laugh, though. "Well, let's not let it."

"It won't," Jenna adds quickly. "So far we've done everything exactly as we were supposed to." She smiles. Then, after consulting the photo one last time, she shifts a few of the objects on the table ever so slightly. "Okay cuz," she says finally. "Sit."

You sit... and you wait. Nothing happens. A full minute of silence goes by. You close your eyes and try to focus, attempting to feel even the slightest, most imperceptible change. No energy surges through you. No ghosts show up. The objects on the table remain exactly where they are, illuminated only by the spectral glow of your propped-up cell phone flashlights.

"We're missing something," you say abruptly.

"What?" the twins ask in stereo.

"I don't know. But something must not be here. There has to be something... else."

On cue a loud noise rumbles into the room, rolling along the broken corridor. It grows more and more familiar as it grinds away.

"The elevator!" Evan cries. "It's moving!"

44

The three of you sprint back to the elevator. Your heart drops the second you realize the doors are closed.

"We're stuck down here!" Evan gasps, glancing around. He's trying to keep it together but his voice is lined with panic. "There's no button to call the elevator back!"

"Someone will see the key sticking out," Jenna reasons. "They'll turn it, and end up here."

Reluctantly you slip the long silver key from your pocket and hold it up. Everyone's shoulders slump. It's one of the few times you wish you weren't so thorough. Then...

"Wait," Jenna says. "It's coming back!"

The grind and screech of ancient cables grows louder as the old elevator rumbles downward. It stops before you in a puff of dust. The doors open... and James Roakes steps out.

"Hello," Mr. Roakes says genially. He's fully dressed now. Under one arm he carries a large mirror with floral accents at the corners. It's the same mirror you noticed hanging in his suite. And also–

"That's the mirror!" Evan cries. "The one from the photograph!"

James Roakes nods. "Yes it is. I thought you could use it." He turns to Jenna, his expression going solemn. "You shamed me young lady," he says. "But you were right. My inaction has been inexcusable, especially considering all that you've done tonight. I need to thank you for that." Jenna smiles, and Mr. Roakes smiles back.

"How do you know about this place?" you ask. "How'd you even get down here?"

The man points backward. A long silver key sticks out of the elevator, identical to your own. "You're not the only one who knows the Aurora's secrets." He brushes past you, still carrying the mirror. "Shall we?"

Back in the ceremony chamber, everything is still arranged. You and Evan hang the mirror carefully, right between the outline of the two bookcases. Mr. Roakes produces a matchbook and lights the oil lamp. He also lights the candle. The illumination makes the room instantly warmer. Brighter.

"Alright," you say, reaching for the back of the chair. "Let me try this again." But before you can sit down, a hand closes over your own. The grip is firm, the voice commanding.

"No," James Roakes says. "It has to be me."

James Roakes takes his seat at the table, looking very much like his great grandfather. The entire scene resembles the photograph so much it's actually spooky.

"Five past one," he says, pulling out an old pocket watch. "Three minutes to go."

You look confused, but this time it's your cousins who have the answer. "That's when the original ceremony took place!" Jenna reasons. "And that's why the old clock in the lobby is stuck on 1:08."

Mr Roakes doesn't respond. He seems to have fallen oddly silent. Abruptly, a wind picks up from out of nowhere. You hear whispers. Voices. They seem to come from all directions, but also, from none.

"It's happening," Evan breathes. "It's–"

He stops mid-sentence as light flares from the ball of crystal in the center of the table. There's some kind of white smoke inside it now, churning slowly, as if somehow alive. The temperature in the room has dropped at least five degrees.

James closes his eyes, extends his arms, and places his hands face down. The second his palms touch the surface of the table, everything moves. The bell shifts over an inch. The candle begins flickering. The book springs open on its own, flipping wildly through its leaves. Moving left and right, it finally settles on a pair of pages.

"Look!" Jenna cries over the rising wind. "The portal!"

46

The light from the oil lamp, reflected in the mirror, is casting an image on the opposite wall. You can see the gateway now. It's a portal of sorts, reaching through space and into a dark, purplish-colored void. Meanwhile, the pure white smoke in the crystal has gone utterly grey. It seems to grow darker with every second that ticks by. You check your phone. 1:07. One minute to show time.

All of a sudden an unseen force strikes you – an intense pressure, shoving you back from the scene at hand. You push back against it, fighting to stay on your feet. To either side of you, Jenna and Evan have been pinned back against opposite walls.

"Fight it!" Evan shouts. "I–I can't..."

You push harder. Turning your body sideways, you knife your way through. You take another step forward and break into the eye of the supernatural hurricane. The candle is still lit. The smoke in the crystal is midnight black. Mr. Roakes is mumbling something unintelligible, his eyes rolled back in his head. There's a deafening roar in your ears. Everything is vibrating.

"Do it Scotty!" you hear Jenna scream. "Do it now!"

Okay, this is it! What do you do?

If you reach forward and ring the bell, *TURN TO PAGE 144*

If you blow out the candle, *SEE WHAT HAPPENS ON PAGE 58*

If you pick up the crystal ball and smash it, *GO TO PAGE 70*

If you lean over and read the book, *HEAD DOWN TO PAGE 114*

You step back as Evan unlocks the door to 109. Almost immediately, your cousin is bathed in crimson.

"This is the red room," he explains. "Another of the Aurora's owners thought it would be fun to do a bunch of rooms in different colors."

You enter the room, your eyes struggling to adjust. Blood-colored walls blend with crimson linens, all set squarely upon a deep red rug. You can't even imagine the kind of person who thought this would be a good idea.

"I never liked this room," Evan says. "Mostly because of the artwork."

It doesn't take long to see what he's talking about. Several paintings are hung about the room, depicting landscapes that seem totally off. The skies are all wrong. The mountains and forests seem warped and twisted. Everything has an almost alien-type feel to it, and not in a cool sci-fi way. To make matters worse, most of the artwork is hung crooked... and in all red frames.

Determined to ignore all this, you commence searching the big scarlet mess. You're about to declare the place empty when you come across an inscription scrawled at the base of one of the paintings:

What you seek lies beneath

"C'mere," you call your cousin over. "Check this out."

Evan reads the inscription with a raised eyebrow and then carefully removes the painting from the wall. There's nothing behind it. There's also nothing between the painting and the frame itself. He sets it aside.

"Beneath, beneath..." you repeat like a mantra. You look down. Evan follows your gaze to the only two things beneath the painting: a decorative bronze vent cover (painted red!) and the trailing edge of the heavy burgundy rug.

"Gotta be one of those," your cousin shrugs.

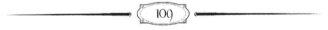

109

If you want to pry loose the vent cover, *FLIP BACK TO PAGE 59*
If you'd rather try rolling back the area rug, *HEAD DOWN TO PAGE 132*

48

You pat your leg. Something hard juts from one of your side pockets.

The ring!

Reaching in, you pull it out. The jewel set into the gold seems almost alive – it's definitely glowing red now. Stepping forward, you pry Mr. Roakes's hand from the table and slip it onto his right ring finger, just like in the photograph. Then something amazing happens.

The light in the mirror projects itself outward, swirling through the glass. It materializes at James Roakes's side, coalescing from a shapeless mass into a much more solid form. The nethergate pulsates. The crystal globe hums, the swirl of shadows now moving at impossibly high speeds. A painful ringing noise assails your ears. It grows higher and higher in pitch and volume until the ball of crystal finally explodes!

Whoa! Quick, *TURN TO PAGE 96*

Quietly, you and Jenna slip into the hotel lounge. Rich mahogany bookcases line the walls here, filled with hundreds – maybe thousands – of old, dusty books. A handy ladder is mounted on slide rails for easy access to the top shelves.

"This was once the Aurora's library," Jenna says unnecessarily, "back when people, you know, read a lot of books."

"Hey, I *still* read books!"

Jenna smirks and waves an arm at the stacks. "Not real books, cuz. Paper ones, anyway." Admittedly she's got you there. Jenna pulls the old photo of Alastair Roakes from her pocket and points to it. "The good news is if this book is anywhere in the hotel, it's probably here."

"And the bad news?"

Your cousin makes her way over to the wooden ladder and shakes it. It doesn't budge.

"Oh."

"Yeah, dad screwed it into the wall a while back. Too many kids were playing with it, and guests weren't using it anyway." Jenna scrambles up a shelf, which bows slightly under her weight. She grabs one of the books at the top, and flips it forward onto its spine. "It's not this one," she declares.

"How do you know?"

Your cousin jumps nimbly down and thrusts the photo into your hand. "Because look. Alastair's book has these thingies on the edges."

"You mean corner-guards?"

Jenna punches you in the arm. "Yeah, those. Smart guy." She slips the photo back in her pocket. "So that's the plan. We turn every book in the library on its edge until we find the one we need. You want me to do the top rows since I'm lighter? Or would you like the honors?"

If you think Jenna should search the top bookshelves, *FLIP TO PAGE 28*

If you'd rather do it yourself and let her search the bottom, *HEAD TO PAGE 131*

50

Bravely you fling open the door and step out into the hall. All the way down, at the opposite end, you can make out a figure just turning the corner. "Come on!" you shout back to Evan. Then you start running.

You tear down the carpeted hall, turn the corner, and pick up speed again. For some reason the hall seems to get longer, not shorter. Gradually it becomes smaller too, more narrow and confined. As the walls seem to be closing in, a strange sense of vertigo slows you down.

Off to one side you pass a strange-looking room marked as 126. There's an old man inside. His mouth is moving, but no sound is coming out. He seems to be pointing upward...

The door slams shut so hard it knocks you to your knees. When you look up again, all the doors are gone. You're in a dead end. Impossibly, both ends of the hall are cut off. The vertigo returns, worse than before.

Darkness seeps in along the edges of your vision.

You're spinning...

Falling...

THE SECRET OF THE AURORA HOTEL

"Scott!" Evan's voice comes from a place that seems muffled and very far away. "Scott, wake up!" Pain flares as your cousin slaps you hard across the face. You reach up with one hand. By the warmth radiating from your cheek, it's probably not the first time he's hit you.

"Oh man, I thought I was losing you!" Evan gasps. "Are you okay? Should I call a doctor?"

"No," you croak. "No, I'm fine. I was just... I...." You rub your eyes. "What happened?"

Evan shakes his head. "You fainted, that's what happened." The hall you're in is very short, with doors lining both sides. Everything looks normal again.

"Did you see the guy in 126?" you ask.

"126?"

"Yeah. He was... weird. Like he was there and not there." Your voice cracks, and Evan hands you a water bottle. You accept it gratefully. "And he was pointing," you continue after downing three huge gulps. "Pointing up. What's up?"

"Third floor," Evan says. "And of course, the roof. You *sure* about the room number?"

You nod your head, and your cousin looks genuinely concerned. "Scott," he says, his voice placating, "there *is* no room 126. After a bunch of construction in the 1950's, the rooms were made bigger on this floor. There hasn't been a room 126 for a really, really long time..."

More ghosts? You bet!

Grab your courage and check the next room when you *TURN TO PAGE 126*

52

The dread overwhelms you. It's just too much. You feel yourself sinking to the floor, only maybe it's your soul that's sinking. As far as your mind is concerned, your body no longer exists.

"Scott!"

From somewhere distant, your cousin screams. Your heart fills with grief, anguish, sorrow – and a whole host of other, more terrible emotions you never knew existed. You can no longer feel yourself breathing. Darkness closes in.

"Scott...."

Evan's voice barely reaches you now. It's like he's a million miles away. He might as well be, because you know with a sudden, frightening certainty you're in a place he can no longer help you.

Whatever happens to be behind the door, you're soon going to face it. Alone. Which means, of course, that this is

---

THE END

You throw Jenna one last skeptical look. Then, moving with deliberate slowness, you push your finger past the broken teeth and into the statue's mouth...

"YAAAHH!!!!"

Jenna's shout is loud, guttural. It scares the absolute daylights out of you! You jerk your arm back reflexively, scraping yourself on the broken stone teeth. A tiny droplet of blood forms on the top of your finger.

Your cousin doesn't even notice. She's too busy laughing.

"Oh man! I can't believe you actually did it!" Her laughter makes you feel all the more foolish, but on seeing your wound her face softens a bit. "Aww, sorry Scotty. I didn't mean for you to get–"

"Forget it," you say bitterly. But then you catch your cousin's gaze and the two of you can't help but burst out laughing again. "Alright. You got me."

"You can get me next time," Jenna says. "Fair's fair. Now come on. Let's hit the lobby."

Check out the lobby *OVER ON PAGE 68*

54

"I guess I'll check the bathroom," you tell Evan. "Call me if you find anything."

You slip inside and flip on the light. It's a pretty standard hotel bathroom, except for the dark wood fixtures that match the rest of the 1970's decor. The tub is empty. The cabinets too. But the mirror...

You lean forward. When you look closely, there appear to be streaks on the mirror's surface. *Or maybe writing.* Instinctively you close the door and twist on the shower, setting the handle to maximum heat. You turn the hot water spigot beneath it on full blast as well, and the room begins to steam up.

Gradually, a message appears in the mirror. The letters appear doubled-up, and when you wipe a finger across them they don't smudge. As if they were traced on the glass from the *inside...*

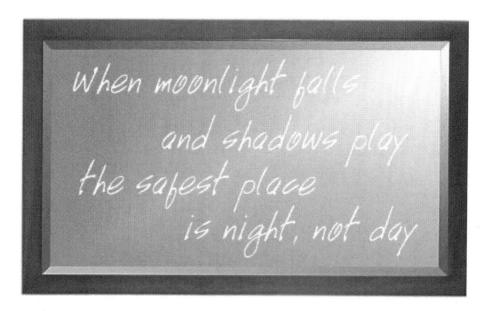

When moonlight falls
and shadows play
the safest place
is night, not day

The door opens and Evan enters with a swirl of steam. "Nothing in there," he says. Your cousin glances up at the mirror. "Whoa..."

"Yeah," you agree. "Better write this one down."

Check out the next room on the manifest when you *TURN TO PAGE 69*

The food makes you uneasy. You are however, thirsty. Maybe just a little drink...

As you pick up the glass, every other ghost at the table does the same. "To Alastair!" the head ghost declares. He stands and lifts his arm in salute. Reflexively, you find yourself doing the same.

Slowly you bring the glass to your lips. The amber liquid is both delicious and refreshing as it slides down your throat. It's so cold it's like drinking liquid ice.

"Fruit juice," Jenna declares. You notice her own glass is already half empty. "Not sure which fruit, though."

Off to the side, something moves. You catch it in your peripheral vision. Turning, you realize it came from the mirror. But rather than see your reflection – or the reflection of everyone else at the table – you see a lone man staring back from beyond the glass.

It's the man from your cousins' photo. Alastair. He looks straight into your eyes as he holds up his left hand; empty palm and empty fingers. He points to it...

"Cuz?"

You blink and the image is gone. Jenna is waving her hand before your eyes, trying to get your attention. She puts down her glass and points to the place settings.

"We eating any of this stuff or no?"

You can try the cream soup by *GOING TO PAGE 135*
You can try the weird salad when you *TURN TO PAGE 65*
You can taste the roast beef by *FLIPPING DOWN TO PAGE 152*
You can also eat nothing. If this is your choice, *GO TO PAGE 64*

56

Room 103 looks as plain and nondescript as a hotel room can get. It's furnished with a mixture of new and old, but there's enough modernization to realize it's been recently updated. There's also a chill in the air here. It makes you wish you'd gone exploring in more than a T-shirt.

"No TV?" you ask. "What kind of place is your dad running here?"

Evan smiles and pulls open a giant armoire. Hidden behind the doors is a flat-screen television. "I'll never understand why people hide TVs like this," he says. "Like they're some dirty little secret or–"

Your cousin stops talking. He stands there, eyes wide, as the apparition of a woman fades into view. She floats toward him, slowly and deliberately. She reaches out...

... and closes the armoire.

You blink once and she's gone.

"D-did you see that!" Evan stutters.

You nod, numbly. Up until now, the only ghosts you've seen have been in movies. But this is *real*. This is...

Evan leans against the wall for support, accidentally knocking a painting crooked. Instantly the woman appears again. She floats over, rights it, then fades quickly away. You'd swear she looks annoyed as she blinks out of existence.

"What the–"

You step up. Open some drawers. You push back the mattress and look under the bed. Each time you touch something, the ghost puts it back. The air gets colder with every movement.

"Come on," you say. You teeth are chattering and you can even see your breath. "Hurry up. We're almost done."

Evan joins you, and eventually you've upended the entire room without finding a single thing. You turn to leave, and when you look back from the doorway it's like you haven't touched anything at all.

103

Cross the hall and enter room 106 when you *TURN TO PAGE 138*

Winding back, you put your arm swiftly and decisively through the window of the cupola. The glass shatters instantly, falling in jagged shards around your feet.

"Nice," Jenna declares. As she reaches in to unlock the door however, you notice she suddenly stops. "Uh oh."

You glance down. The top of Evan's sweatshirt is blossoming bright red. Slowly you unwrap your arm and your worst fears are realized: there's a long, deep cut across the top of your forearm.

"Quick, put pressure on it," Evan says. You try clamping your hand over the cut but it's too long. Droplets of blood fall from either side of your hand, painting tiny red beads in the snow. "Oh man," your cousin laments.

The cut is going to need a whole bunch of stitches. And sooner, rather than later. All of this is very unfortunate, because you really were getting somewhere!

For now though, I'm afraid your night of solving the Aurora's mysteries has come to

THE END

58

The noise, the wind, the glow of the portal – it's just too much! You screw your eyes closed against the chaos. When you open them again, the candle is still flickering before you. Instinctively you lean forward and blow it out...

Everything stops.

The light, the wind, the intense cold – all of it is gone in the span of an instant. The book slams shut on itself. The crystal goes from black, to grey, to white... and then to nothing at all. It's only a piece of glass now, sitting in the middle of an old table. Still hanging from the ceiling, the oil lamp sways gently back and forth.

James Roakes's eyes flip open. They shift in your direction. "What happened?"

"I–I blew out the candle," you say.

His face goes instantly pale. "And why did you do that?"

Your stomach falls out from under you, like the first drop on a roller coaster. "I... I just..."

Mr. Roakes stands. He lets out the longest, saddest sigh you've ever heard. "The spirits of the hotel," he explains, "were trapped in the crystal here. We could have sent them through the nethergate, delivering them back to a place they would be at peace. Instead, you ended the ceremony prematurely." He looks around forlornly down at the table. "Now they're stranded at the Aurora once more."

You sink your face into your palms as Evan and Jenna step behind you. A comforting hand finds its way to your shoulder.

"There's always next year, cuz," Jenna says. Her attempt at cheering you up is still undermined with disappointment. "Right?"

Mr. Roakes shrugs. "Perhaps," he says. "Perhaps not. That force you felt was Warrick, the worst spirit of them all. We surprised him this time, and I think that's why we escaped with our lives. But next year, he'll be ready. Next time, we might not be so lucky."

Evan squeezes your shoulder consolingly. "Doesn't matter," he says firmly. "We're still gonna try."

Well, as Jenna said there's always next year. Hopefully, the Aurora will still be in business. But for the next twelve long months, this looks like

THE END

You kneel down before the vent cover. Hand-poured bronze, it depicts two scrolling interlocking hearts. At one time, it was probably very beautiful. Someone totally ruined it by painting it red.

Behind the cover is a recessed area shrouded in darkness.

"We're in luck," you say. "There aren't any screws."

The only thing holding the vent cover to the wall is a thick layer of red paint. You work some of it away with a fingernail, then begin pulling at the top two corners. It still doesn't budge.

"Come on," Evan teases. "You can pull harder than that!"

You curl your fingertips around the edge and pull harder. Slowly the thick coating of latex paint begins stretching in your direction...

Okay champ, roll a single die.

If you rolled a 1 or a 5, *TURN TO PAGE 29*

If you rolled a 2, 3, 4, or 6, *GO TO PAGE 86*

60

With your cousin on your shoulders it's very hard to look up. You're kind of winging it.

"Grab that first one," you tell her.

Jenna reaches for the candle, stretching as far as her body will go. You feel the muscles in her legs go tight for a second, and your heart jumps into your throat. She's going to fall!

"Wait!" you cry. You try conjuring a mental image of the photo again. "No, not that one." You grip her ankles with both hands now, using only your shins to steady yourself on the ladder. It hurts.

"It's one of the other ones," you say through gritted teeth. "I'm sure of it."

Make another choice:

If you tell Jenna to grab candle number 2, *TURN TO PAGE 110*

If you tell Jenna to grab candle number 3, *TURN TO PAGE 158*

You reach into your pocket and pull out the small pewter cannon. Evan looks on in disbelief.

"We found this downstairs," you say, handing it over to him. "In the lobby."

Evan studies the board for a long moment, then carefully places the cannon on one of the squares.

Immediately there's a change. The apparition of the young man flutters and glows brightly. He reaches out, takes the cannon, and moves it into a new position. Then he sits back and actually smiles.

"The missing piece was a knight," Evan explains. "And that's checkmate."

The ghost of the young man stands up abruptly and faces Evan. There's a look of triumph on the apparition's face, but also, gratitude.

"*Don't read the book*," the ghost whispers, laying a glowing hand on your cousin's shoulder. Then it bows to him with a flourish, and disappears.

The three of you stand in silence for a moment. It's Jenna who finally speaks.

"Um, did a ghost just pat you on the shoulder?" she asks her brother.

"I– I think so."

Jenna grins. "This is the best Halloween *ever!*"

Nice work right there! Head out the window and onto the frozen roof when you
FLIP DOWN TO PAGE 150

62

You watch as Evan unlocks the door to room 116. There's a strange haze that hangs in the air here, even after flipping on all the lights.

"We should do this room quickly," Evan says. Although he's trying to stay casual, you can detect a certain edge to his voice.

"Why?"

"No reason," he fibs. After a quick frown from you however, he relents. "Fine," your cousin sighs. "Everyone who stays in here ends up switching their room. They won't always say why. It's gotten to the point where dad won't rent it unless we're all filled up."

You nod to let him know you appreciate the honesty. "The Aurora fills up? Well that's cool. I thought the hotel was struggling?"

"It is," Evan admits. "But sometimes when there's an event, or a convention–"

The conversation halts as an apparition materializes between you. Shockingly, by now neither of you are surprised. You and Evan stand there, watching as the ghostly white form of an elderly man comes into focus. He appears to be fussing with a pair of wire-rimmed spectacles.

"Scott–"

"Shh!" you hiss, silencing you cousin. A moment later the apparition begins to move. It flutters weirdly in the dim haze, its movements halting or even jerky at times. It makes you feel like you're watching an old reel-to-reel movie, but a couple of frames of film are missing. The ghost heads toward the window, stops, then changes direction. Without slowing down, it floats right through the wall.

"What the–"

Ignoring your cousin, you push over to where the apparition disappeared. A large vanity table blocks the wall. You slide it backward and start pressing against the wall with your hand. As you suspected, there's a narrow gap where the wallpaper bows inward.

"There was a door here," you say excitedly. "But they covered it."

Evan looks back at you nervously. "Maybe they had a reason to?"

"Or maybe someone's hiding something," you say. Using your fingertips, you can make out the edges of a narrow doorway. It's just big enough to enter, but you'd have to rip the paper to go through.

116

Do you follow the ghost? If you really are that brave, *FLIP BACK TO PAGE 33*
Follow a ghost? Are you nuts? To head back into the hallway, *PLAY IT SAFE ON PAGE 108*

"Alright," you tell Jenna. "I'm with you." Your cousin sticks her tongue out at her brother before beaming back at you. "Evan, we'll meet up with you afterward. Just be careful."

"You too," he says. "And try to keep a low profile down there. The lobby level will have more people awake."

You nod and head out into the hallway. The first floor is a silent, carpeted world that stretches in two directions.

"The Grand Staircase is down that way," Jenna points. She pops a piece of pink gum in her mouth. "Or if you want, we can take *that.*"

Your cousin jerks her head toward the hotel's inner glass elevator. It looks old and rickety, but it's also really, really cool.

You can take the Grand Staircase by *TURNING TO PAGE 128*
Or you can jump in the glass elevator *OVER ON PAGE 37*

64

A thought occurs to you: if the ghosts are over a hundred years old, maybe the food is too. And the idea of eating century-old ghost-food doesn't sound very appealing.

"I think I'm gonna skip this meal," you tell Jenna. "Besides," you say, rubbing your stomach, "your dad already fed us earlier."

Jenna stares back at you, obviously crushed. She looks like a kid who opened her biggest birthday present to find nothing inside.

"Not very adventurous, cuz," she tells you. "And here I thought we were on an *actual* adventure."

There are two exits leading out of the dining hall.

To head into the Aurora's lounge area, *TURN TO PAGE 49*

If you'd rather check out the hotel kitchen, *GO TO PAGE 117*

If you're trying anything, you decide it's going to be the salad. I mean, how bad could a salad be?

You switch utensils and slide it over, and for once your cousin follows your lead. Your fork slides through the phantom greens with an unexpected crunch. When you lift it to your mouth, something doesn't seem right. Something's moving!

"Ugh!" Jenna cries, throwing her own fork down. Skewered at the end is what looks like a tiny tentacle! It writhes and twists on the ghostly table as you throw your own fork away in revulsion.

"I'm open to trying new things," Jenna cries, "but this is crossing the line! Come on, Scotty. Let's go!"

For some reason you nod apologetically to the ghost seated across from you before hopping out of your chair. After dabbing its chin with a napkin, you receive a firm nod back. Then Jenna is whisking you away, pulling you through a large opening and into the next room.

"Next time we check the menu first," your cousin says. "Because that was ridiculous."

Yuck! Well, almost anyway. Looks like you've avoided the grossness for now.
You can head into the hotel lounge *OVER ON PAGE 49*
Or check out the Aurora's kitchen by *TURNING TO PAGE 117*

66

You leave the weeping woman behind you and slip through the adjoining door. The next room is a mirror image of the previous one, as so often happens with hotel suites. Only this one appears totally bare.

"It's dark in here," Jenna declares. Since the light switch is on the other side of the room, she pulls open the curtains and lets the moonlight spill in.

Right away you notice something interesting. A large steel checkerboard has been welded over the window, preventing exit. The squares of metal – and lack thereof – throw mismatched shadows of light and dark across the floor of the empty room.

"Hey, just like hopscotch!" your cousin coos. She gets up on one leg and prepares to jump...

You drop a hand on Jenna's shoulder. "Hang on a second." Extending an arm, you point out the alternating pattern of moonlight and shadow. "There's a reason the floor looks like this. There has to be."

You can tell by Evan's body language that he seems to agree with you. "Yeah, I think so too," he nods. "But what?"

214

If you tell Jenna to step only on the moonlit squares, *TURN TO PAGE 82*
If you instruct her to stay on the shadow squares instead, *GO TO PAGE 18*

The footsteps, you realize, are coming from the left. And off to the right, you don't like the sound of the machine at all.

"Backtrack," you say quickly.

"What?"

"We need to go back," you tell Jenna. "Now, before somebody sees us!"

Before your cousin can say anything you grab her wrist and pull her back down the hallway. The noises get louder just as you reach the end, slipping around the corner before you're seen. It's a good thing you're decisive!

Backtrack to the lobby and enter the Aurora's dining area *OVER ON PAGE 102*

68

Together, you and Jenna move into the lobby. At this hour the big area is empty and desolate, save for a single blue-haired woman standing behind the front desk. An old clock built into the molding behind her seems stopped on the wrong time of 1:08.

"That's Agnes," Jenna says. "Don't mind her. She's half deaf and partially blind." Your cousin scratches her head. "Or is it mostly deaf and half blind? I can never remember."

The room itself is impressive. Long columns stretch to an arched ceiling three stories high. Beyond the clinical couches and uniform seating areas the place is still warm and inviting, possibly because of the tremendous fireplace built into the opposite wall. Even at this hour, its flames are still roaring.

Presiding over the lobby on the upper floors is an ornate wrap-around landing. For a second you think you see someone up there, leaning over the rail. But when you look again more closely, all you can make out are shadows.

You turn back to find your cousin creeping like a ninja toward the front desk. She arrives unseen, crouched against the facade, one finger pressed to her lips in a "shushing" gesture.

"AGNES!" Jenna cries, leaping up into view. The old woman is so startled her glasses actually fly off her face. They end up dangling by a chain around her neck.

"WHAT? Who? Oh... Jenna! What are you doing up at this–"

"My father would like your help in the kitchen," she says sweetly. "Please."

"The kitchen? At this hour? What could–"

"I don't know," Jenna shrugs. She takes a single flower from a nearby vase and tucks it into her hair. "But it sounded pretty urgent."

You watch as the woman nods, composes herself, and eventually exits the lobby. "That was mean," you tell your cousin. "Really mean."

"Yeah probably," Jenna agrees. "But it got her out of here, didn't it?"

The lobby is all yours for the taking! What will you do first?

There's a side room filled with what appears to be an old taxidermy display. To check it out, *TURN TO PAGE 112*

Behind the front desk is the manager's office. You can search that room by *GOING TO PAGE 16*

Or you can check out the fireplace and surrounding area. Do that *OVER ON PAGE 77*

With the click of another lock you enter room 119. Instantly your eyes go wide, because the room is entirely blue. The walls are blue. The floor is blue. Even the ceiling is... well, blue. It's the strangest thing you've ever seen.

"More theme rooms?"

"Yeah," Evan says. "Colors, this time. Dad's getting around to redecorating them, but sometime people ask for these. Quirky, I guess." He picks up a blue throw pillow and drops it back on a blue suede couch. "There used to be an orange room, if you can believe that. But people said it gave them pounding headaches, so..."

Some of the room's decor is off color, but not by much. You get busy checking a navy blue chest of drawers. Evan rifles through a sky blue night table. Eventually you've searched the entire room without finding anything. But one item does stand out: a smooth, three-foot long elephant tusk stands upright in one corner. It looks weirdly out of place.

"That thing's not blue," you say, pointing to it.

Evan looks over his shoulder and shrugs. "What can I say? This place is kooky." He unlocks an adjoining blue door in one wall. "Here, this leads to 121. The white room, if I remember it right." He laughs. "I know, I know, *very* exciting. In fact–"

BANG! BANG! BANG!

You both whirl at the sound. The three sharp knocks originated from the door you just entered through. Quietly you step over and peer through the peephole. The hallway appears empty.

Quick, what do you do?

If you throw open the door to the hallway, *TURN TO PAGE 50*

If you'd rather slip through the suite door and into the next room, *HEAD TO PAGE 126*

70

The crystal ball seems to be the center of everything. It's swirling madly now, the darkness inside moving with dizzying speed. Wispy, shadow-like tendrils arc outward like fingers reaching from an inky black core.

You pick it up. In contrast to the icy cold of the room, the ball of glass is incredibly warm in your hand. Within it you can almost feel... life. The voices grow louder, and in an alarming instant you realize those voices are all coming from inside your head.

Holding it overhead you pause, and then finally heave the ball downward. It smashes spectacularly against the cobblestone floor. You shield your eyes as shards of glass fly in every direction. At the point of impact, a dark spiral of black smoke is all that remains.

The voices in your head scream all at once, but this time the screams sound triumphant. One by one tendrils of smoke spin off across the room. They disappear into the nethergate, as if drawn by some invisible, irresistible whirlpool operating at its center. Eventually, there's only one thread left. The last one, much darker than the rest, seems to resist being pulled away. But it can't fight forever. With what sounds like a gut-wrenching shriek, it too disappears into the void.

Everything stops at once. The noise, the wind, even the cold. You're suddenly aware of the room again. Whatever was holding Evan and Jenna abruptly releases them.

"What..." Evan gasps. "What just happened?"

You blink a few times to clear your vision. "I don't know. Mr. Roakes, what did we–"

There's a groan as James Roakes stirs from where he rests face down on the table. Jenna hurries over and helps him to a sitting position. He rubs his eyes for what seems like forever before finally opening them again. When he notices the crystal ball is missing he turns to you curiously.

"Did you..."

"He shattered it," Jenna confirms. "Yes." Her nose twitches trying to gauge the man's reaction.

Did you do the right thing? Or did you mess everything up?

Much to your relief, Mr. Roakes breaks into a smile.

"So uh," Evan starts warily, "what exactly just happened?"

Mr. Roakes clears his throat. "Long ago," he begins, "this hotel was plagued by restless spirits. My great grandfather considered himself a medium of sorts. He traveled to the Aurora in order to help put those souls at rest." He gestures to the objects still on the table. "The ceremony Alastair was performing was designed to open a gateway. One that would allow these spirits to travel to their next place in the universe."

"But he failed, right?" Jenna jumps in. "He never got the chance to finish?"

James shakes his head. "I wouldn't say he *failed*, but you're exactly right. The ceremony was never finished. The gateway was left open, but only partially. This allowed even more spirits to enter the Aurora and become stuck here."

"Why did he fail?" you ask. "What happened?"

"And who's Warrick?" Evan adds.

"Ah, Warrick." You can't help but notice Mr. Roakes shudder visibly at the name. "Most of the spirits were harmless, but not him. Of his life we know little, but his was an angry demise. For reasons unknown, he was bound to this place from the very beginning. Since even before the hotel was built."

Jenna gulps. "And now?"

"And now," James sighs, "he's gone too. Passed through the portal, along with all of the others. Even Alastair." The man turns to face you and smiles. "The Aurora is safe now, thanks to you. It is no longer a place of sorrow."

"You mean it's no longer haunted?" Evan asks.

"Yes," Mr. Roakes chuckles. "That's one way to put it."

72

Your cousins look at each other and smile. For a split-second you think they might even hug, but then Jenna blows another bubble. "Well," she says, "dad's going to love that. It'll be good for business."

A thought suddenly crosses your mind. "Know what's even better for business?" you ask.

Your two cousins stare back at you, not sure what to expect.

"Ghost tours!"

Evan opens his mouth, presumably to say something sarcastic. You cut him off. "No, really! Think about it. This place has *the* most haunted history of any hotel ever. Lots of people *love* that!"

"They do?" Evan asks.

"Yeah," Jenna confirms. "They actually do."

"Now you can have all the spooky appeal of a haunted hotel," you continue, "without the actual danger of some nethergate still being open. Uncle Gus– I mean, your dad can use the Aurora's past to his advantage."

Your cousins look contemplative. It's certainly something to consider.

As the four of you head to the elevator, you cast one final glance backward. Maybe it's just a trick of the light, but you swear you still see a glimmer in the mirror. A tiny spark, somewhere deep in the glass...

Congratulations on saving your uncle's hotel! You're sure to have lots more adventures with Evan and Jenna, but for now this is very happily

THE END

You don't want to risk breaking whatever happens to be in the vase. Evan looks on as you reach inside...

OUCH!

Something bites you!

You leap back, startled, clutching your hand. As you do, the vase tips over. A humongous centipede slithers out, feeling the air with its antennae for a moment before scurrying away. Evan gasps.

"Did it–"

"Bite me? Yeah." Apprehensively, you look down. On the back of your hand, a nasty red welt is rising up. A thick droplet of blood oozes forth, running down toward your fingers.

"At least you're not allergic," your cousin speculates. His expression goes grave. "*Are* you?"

You don't answer. You've never been bitten by a centipede before, but already the skin around the wound is turning an angry purple. Your hand no longer stings. Where there was pain just a minute ago, now you can barely feel anything.

"Flex your fingers."

You do what Evan tells you. Or at least, you try to. Your whole hand has gone totally numb! You can't move it, or flex it, or anything at all. Your cousin's look of worry tells the rest of the story.

"I'm... fine..." you say. But the wooziness is undeniable. You struggle to keep upright, but then Evan is there to catch you as your legs give out. It's time to see a doctor. Fast.

Well, at least now you know you're allergic to bug bites. The bad news however, is that it makes this

THE END

74

Chucking things up at the chandelier sounds noisy and risky. As much as you hate to admit it, the ladder seems like the safer choice. "Let's see how high this thing will get us," you say.

Jenna helps you set up directly beneath the candelabra. Carefully you climb to the second to last step and stretch your arms upward. The candles are almost within reach... but not quite.

"I'm coming up," Jenna says. You feel the ladder creak beneath her added weight. She climbs over your back, grabbing your head for leverage. At one point she leans too far forward and has to dig in to keep her balance. You end up with a thumb in your mouth. "Oops! Sorry Scotty!"

"Just go slow," you say, wincing. "Real slow."

Finally she's in position, legs over your shoulders. *This is crazy,* you think. But it's already done. You do your best to keep Jenna stable while using your hands to grip the ladder. It feels like your whole body is shaking.

"Almost there!" your cousin says. "I just need to stretch a little bit more..."

You raise your chin slightly and dare to look up. The candles are close now. Three of them seem older, more yellowed than the rest. They also have markings on them.

"Which one do I take?" Jenna calls down to you.

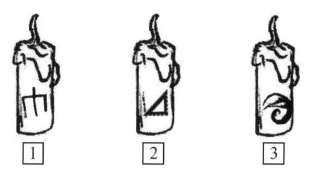

If you tell Jenna to take candle number 1, *TURN TO PAGE 60*
If you tell Jenna to take candle number 2, *TURN TO PAGE 110*
If you tell Jenna to take candle number 3, *TURN TO PAGE 158*

76

Evan stands frozen, looking over your shoulder and out the strange window. He hasn't even answered you.

"Well *I'm* stepping out," you say defiantly. "You can stay here if you want."

Carefully you pull yourself through the window and step onto the ledge. The Aurora's fancy stone facade holds your weight easily, even if there isn't much room to maneuver. Right away you're struck with how bright everything is. High up in the sky, the sun is a muted yellow coin the size of a dime.

That can't be, you think. *It's after midnight.*

The weird desert landscape stretches all the way to the horizon. You see nothing but cracked earth and mounds of sand. Directly below you, a dune has piled high enough against the side of the hotel you can almost reach out and touch it. If you were to hang from the ledge by your fingertips, you could drop into the sand and go exploring.

"Scott!" Evan's voice sounds dull and muted from inside the room. He pokes his head out nervously and calls again. "Scott, get back in here! This isn't... right."

You look back one last time and think you see something poking up from the sand. Something white.

"Scott, come on!"

You're torn. You want to investigate further, but you're also not sure you could get back up to the ledge once you dropped. And hey, maybe Evan's right after all. Maybe.

Do you drop down from the ledge? If so, *FLIP TO PAGE 159*
Or do you climb back in through the window? *GO TO PAGE 20*

A sprawling fireplace dominates the rear of the main lobby, surrounded by couches on a plush area rug. The temperature rises pleasantly as you approach, driving away any last trace of chill in the air.

"Here look at this," Jenna says as she runs a hand over the stonework. Her palm stops on a cornerstone, deeply etched with writing:

The Aurora, 1903

"Pretty cool, huh?" she says. "Told you this place was old."

You nod, scanning the area for clues. The hearth, shelf, the mantle – all of it is worn and well-used, but also well taken care of. Without warning, the fire flickers. A blast of cold air blows over you, causing the flames to dance wildly in the firebox.

"*You... will never...*" The whisper is low and barely audible – more of a growl, really. One look into Jenna's face tells you that she hears it too. *"have... what's mine!"*

Another blast of air forces you instinctively backward. The flames settle again, and the air returns to normal. But when you look to Jenna, she's holding something large in her hand. It's the cornerstone from the fireplace.

"It... it was loose!" she stammers. "I didn't mean to take it. I just stumbled backward and–"

"Hang on," you say. In the depression created by the missing stone, something glimmers. You reach inside and pull out a small pewter figurine, in the shape of a cannon. It could be a toy, or maybe a chess piece.

"Who do you think put this in there?" you say. You turn the figure over a few times before dropping it in your pocket.

"Whoever it was, they're long gone by now," Jenna answers. Carefully she replaces the cornerstone. "Come on," she says. "Let's keep moving."

Straight ahead is the hotel's main hall. To continue the search there, *TURN TO PAGE 133*

You can also check out the Aurora's dining room. If so *HEAD OVER TO PAGE 102*

78

You're not sure what the square hole is for, and there's no time to find out. Already the cold is making your fingers numb. Evan is shaking.

"Follow Jenna," you tell your cousin. "I'll be right behind you."

You start the ascent, trying to ignore the fact that the handholds are more icy than you originally thought. You also try not to look down. While you're not terrified of heights, like Evan, you're not too crazy about them either.

"Almost there," Jenna calls down. "Just a few more–"

It happens fast. Evan's left hand slips, then his right. He falls straight into you, butting you away from the wall. You fall.

"Evan! Scotty!"

Jenna's cry is muffled by the storm. It's almost peaceful as you fall end over end, tumbling downward into the swirling snow...

Maybe if you're lucky you'll hit a snowbank. Hey, it happens all the time. But for right now at least, this seems to be

THE END

THE SECRET OF THE AURORA HOTEL

You turn to face Jenna. Tears stream down both of your cousin's cheeks. You wipe them away gently with the back of your hand, then pluck the pretty flower from behind her ear.

The woman stirs and looks over at you. You offer her the flower. A smile spreads over her face as she takes it.

"Wow cuz!" Jenna cries happily. "Nice thinking!"

The ghost-woman bows her head at you gracefully. When she looks up again, she wears a beautiful smile. You feel suddenly warm. Euphoric. You're overcome with the urge to reach out and embrace her, but before you can do that she floats away.

Before leaving the room however, the woman gazes back at you one last time. Her hand goes up, and she points to something on the wall. Then she disappears.

"Whoa," Evan breathes. He's back now, but still recovering.

Your own eyes are locked on the wall, and soon you're examining the place the woman indicated. High up on the printed wallpaper, a pudgy little cherub is ringing a bell.

"Yuck!" Jenna shudders from over your shoulder. "Ghosts I can handle. But cherubs are creepy."

There's a suite door here leading into the adjoining room. Check it out *OVER ON PAGE 66*

80

"Go talk to him," you tell Jenna. "But do it quickly. And quietly."

Jenna delivers her brother an 'I told you so' smirk before slipping around the corner. Evan on the other hand, is staring back at you. He doesn't look pleased.

"Look, maybe he'll listen to her," you say. "Your sister has a certain way with people."

"Yeah," your cousin says. "That's what I'm afraid of."

A minute ticks by. Then two. You're about to go look for Jenna when she comes gliding back, a long silver key spinning from her finger. "Piece of cake," she smiles.

"How'd you get it?" you ask.

Jenna shrugs. "I just told him what we were doing and he gave it to me. Said he didn't even know what the key was for."

Evan looks stunned. "You *told* him? And he just *gave* it to you?"

"Yeah," Jenna says. "Don't forget, Vincent's been here longer than any of us. He knows there are lots of things going on in this place. Oh, and he told me to be careful. Of Warrick."

"Warrick?" Evan asks. "Who's that?"

"I'm willing to bet," you say, "it's the guy in the letter. The *him* Alastair keeps referring to." You return to the elevator and take the key from Jenna. It fits perfectly into the silver keyhole. There's a muffled *click* as you turn it, and the elevator begins rumbling downward.

"If Alastair is afraid of him," Evan says, "then we'd better be *really* careful."

Find out what's *under* the basement when you *TURN TO PAGE 42*

You unwrap Evan's sweatshirt from your arm and hand it back to him. Jenna looks utterly disappointed.

"Umm," you say to her, "aren't you forgetting about something?"

Jenna looks confused. You make a motion toward her pocket. She reaches in and pulls out a tiny, square-shaped key. It's the one she swiped from the janitor's closet.

"Oh yeah!" she cries happily. "I forgot all about this thing!"

You try to smile as Jenna unlocks the cupola, but your face is way too frozen. When the door swings open you can't get inside fast enough.

Sweet! Now get out of the wind and warm yourself up a bit *OVER ON PAGE 88*

82

You look to the places where the moonlight touches the floor. Maybe those squares are safe, you reason. Maybe that's why they're lit up.

"Stick to the moonlit squares," you tell Jenna. "Don't step on the shadow."

Your cousin nods and steps forward. Her foot slips into the moonlight, bearing down on the first illuminated square. Nothing happens. She hops to the second square, the third, the fourth – everything goes smoothly and without incident. You're about to chide yourself for being too cautious when you hear a faint, muffled *click*.

"What was that?" Evan asks nervously.

Jenna freezes, arms extended outward to keep her balance. "I don't know. It happened on that last step, though."

A grinding noise reaches your ears. It grows in volume, filling the room until it's a deafening roar. The floor trembles. Evan clutches the wall as Jenna is thrown to her knees.

"Help!"

The floor drops out from under you. Or rather, it tilts alarmingly in one direction. The three of you are flung involuntarily sideways, sliding along its length until you're deposited into darkness. The floor then pivots back into position above you, trapping you in the space beneath.

"We're stuck!" Jenna cries. You hear her pounding against the ceiling but you can't see anything. Dust fills your nose as you sneeze in the pitch blackness.

"We'll never get out of here!" Evan shouts. You can hear the panic in his voice. Apparently he's got a healthy dose of claustrophobia to go along with his fear of heights. "We'll be trapped down here forever!"

"I doubt it," you say between sneezes. "Did you hear that noise? It must've woken up the whole hotel!" You sneeze again. "I'm sure your father will be here in a matter of minutes."

That last thought sends a wave of dread through you. Then again, explaining things to Uncle Gus sounds a whole lot better than being stuck under a hotel floor for the rest of your life.

Either way, this is certainly

THE END

You crouch there, pinned against the dish washing machine. A few long seconds tick by, and then Jenna grabs your hand and pulls you out into the open.

"Come on, if we move fast we can– *UMPF!*" The two of you run full force into a big, stocky giant of a man.

"Jenna!" the man says. He crosses his arms, which you notice are thick and muscular and covered in hair. "And what might *you* be doing here?"

"I– I um, we... we were–"

"You were looking to steal some more brownies, no doubt." The man glares down at her in apparent anger, but you detect the thin hint of a smirk lying just behind his scowl.

"No!" Jenna protests. You kick her leg. "Er, I mean, yes. Yes, we were!" With a smile your cousin shifts from shock and surprise into her usual warmth and charm. The change is deviously effortless. "I'm sorry Marco. You made them so good the last time, we couldn't help but want more. Evan told me he smelled them again, so he sent me down to–"

The man holds up a hand to stop her. "I figured as much," he says. "Listen you can't be down here. The kitchen is dangerous, especially at night." His eyes shift to you. "And who's this?"

"This is Scotty," she says. "He's our cousin. He's staying the night." Feebly you offer your hand but Marco makes no attempt to take it.

"If your father knew you were down here, know who'd get in trouble?" Marco asks. "Me. Not you," he says pointing a thick finger at Jenna's nose, "just me."

"Sorry," Jenna apologizes again. "We'll head back upstairs now. Quietly. Dad won't even know we were in here."

"He'd better not," Marco chides her. "Or there won't be any more brownies for anyone." Jenna lowers her eyes even further, and this finally seems to satisfy the chef. With a grunt he turns and walks through a set of swinging doors.

Quick – follow Jenna out of the kitchen before anyone else shows up!
TURN TO PAGE 49

84

The knob is frozen beneath your fingers, cold as a block of dry ice. Your heart sinks as you feel trepidation beyond anything you've ever experienced. But also, something else: an underlying sense of awe...

"Scott!"

Suddenly your hand is off the doorknob and you're struggling to regain your balance. Evan has kicked his leg upward, hard, driving your arm away.

"Scott! Are you okay?" he asks. He puts a steadying hand on your shoulder. "Are– Are you crying?"

"No," you say, wiping away tears. "I mean yes. I mean... I'm not really sure." The incredible sadness is still with you, but thankfully it's dissipating. In the back of your mind, you can feel it draining away.

"What just happened?"

"I don't know," you tell your cousin as you take a giant step backward. "But that's *not* the door."

Whew! That was close! Hopefully you pick a better door this time:

If you try the *RED* door, *TURN TO PAGE 22*

If you try the *BLUE* door, *TURN TO PAGE 106*

If you try the *GREEN* door, *TURN TO PAGE 136*

If you try the *GOLD* door, *TURN TO PAGE 145*

You spring forward, reaching for the falling candle. It strikes the tips of your fingers... and you manage to cradle it in a spectacular diving catch!

"Right on, Scotty!" Jenna cheers. Probably a little too loudly, because she immediately covers her mouth with one hand.

Gingerly you get up from the floor. The candle is old, yellowed, maybe crafted from beeswax or who knows what. Marked with a jagged triangle, it looks exactly like the one in the photo.

"I can't believe you caught that," Jenna says.

"Of course I caught it," you brag. "I have the reflexes of a hockey goalie!"

Your cousin's expression turns to one of admiration. "You're a goalie, too? That's cool!"

"Yeah well... no, I'm not. Not *really.*"

Jenna looks back in you in confusion. Then she laughs. "You're weird, cuz." She notices the floor is littered with a giant mess of broken candles. "That was noisy. We gotta go."

Great job! You found the candle!

The lower floor is pretty much picked over. Better go meet up with Evan.

TURN TO PAGE 157

86

You pull back, leaning your full weight into the effort. There's an oddly satisfying rending sound, and then the grate pops free!

It takes a lot of effort to stay on your feet, but somehow you manage. Before discarding the vent cover you notice how jaggedly sharp some of its edges are. Whew! It's a good thing you didn't cut yourself!

"Let's see what's inside," Evan says. He pulls out his cell phone and actives the flashlight. The two of you spend the next minute peering into a very dusty and very empty piece of ductwork.

"Can't win em' all," you shrug. You take your time replacing the painted bronze cover, being careful not to slice your hand open. By the time you're finished, it's hard to tell it was ever removed at all.

Might as well check out the rug too, right? *HEAD OVER TO PAGE 132*

"Vincent!" you cry, suddenly remembering. "He has the key!"

Evan regards you strangely. "Vincent? The janitor?"

"Yeah," Jenna confirms. "We ran into him earlier. But I don't remember him having–"

"He has it," you say. "I saw a long silver key on his key ring that looked really old. Very out of place from the others." You tap the keyhole. "I'll bet it would fit right here."

It's all Jenna needs. She punches the button to the lobby and the elevator starts to move. "You guys stay here," she says. "I'll get it from him."

"You'll *what?*" Evan doesn't look so convinced. "How?"

"He'll just give it to me," Jenna says. "Trust me. Vincent knows what we're doing tonight."

"You *told* him?"

"Yes," you tell Evan. "We did. And he was cool about it. Actually, he was very helpful."

The doors open and Jenna silently disappears into the lobby. You and Evan wait for what seems like forever, but actually turns out to be less than five minutes. When Jenna returns you breathe a sigh of relief – spinning from her finger is a long silver key with teeth on both sides. She presses it into your hand as she steps into the elevator.

"Cross your fingers," you say. The key slips easily into the keyhole, disappearing all the way to the hilt. You turn it clockwise, hard, and are rewarded with a deep, satisfying *click*.

The elevator shakes, then rumbles downward. The three of you look at each other as it descends past the basement and continues onward.

"I hope this is it," Evan says.

"It'd better be," Jenna answers, stuffing another paper wrapper into her pocket. "I'm almost out of gum."

Will Jenna run out of gum?

Find the answer to this and more when you *FLIP TO PAGE 42*

88

The cupola is freezing, but at least you're out of the wind. Jenna closes the door behind her as the three of you huddle together.

"Okay," you say, glad not to have to shout anymore. "What's our next move?"

Your cousins answer with silence. Jenna stares back at you blankly. Evan is busy breathing warm air into his fists.

"Come on," you urge. "One of you has to have an idea. Something? Anything?"

Evan holds his hands out apologetically. "Alastair told us to go up," he says. As he speaks his breath comes out as puffs of white air. "Well, we did. Look at where we are. You don't get any more up than this."

You turn to Jenna, hoping for something more useful. To your surprise, she's grinning like the Cheshire cat.

"Up," she says, pointing. "Look."

You and Evan tilt your chins in unison Directly above you, dangling from the highest part of the cupola's ceiling, is an antique oil lamp.

"Is that–"

"The one from the photograph," Evan confirms. "Sure is."

It takes a boost from your cousin, but you're easily able to reach the lamp. You take it down gingerly, chain and all. Incredibly, it still has oil in it.

"Is there a way down from here?" you ask Evan.

He nods. "Best bet is the fire escape on the east end of the roof. The door at the corner stairwell is never locked. That would put us back on the second floor."

"Why?" Jenna asks. "Where are we going now?"

"To the basement," you answer. The storm is finally dying. You can even see the twinkle of a few stars. "It's time to finish this."

If getting back indoors sounds great right about now, *HEAD TO PAGE 156*

Evan produces the master key and unlocks the door to room 205. It swings open heavily, into a room illuminated by filtered moonlight.

"It's musty in here," Jenna says. She's right. There's a distinct smell to the room that reminds you of an old library.

CLACK!

The three of you turn simultaneously at the sound of the door closing behind you. Only there's one problem. The door is gone!

"This is crazy," you sigh in exasperation. "What in the world made your father buy this place?"

Jenna chuckles. "It grew on him," she answers. "Or at least that's what he told us the first time he brought us up here." Your cousin runs a hand over the wall where the door used to be. "You gotta admit, at least it's not boring."

You'd answer, but you're suddenly overcome with a falling sensation. Only you feel like you're falling *up.* Or maybe everything you think is up is actually falling down on you. It's really hard to explain.

"What's happening?" Evan asks shakily. He's starting to look nauseous. "Are you guys feeling–"

"Yes," Jenna answers. "And I think the walls are moving. Or maybe we're moving and the walls are standing still. Or everything's moving and the hotel is laughing at us. Pick one."

You swallow hard, forcing yourself to stay calm. The door, the windows, even the furniture – everything in the room is gone. It's a clean slate, a blank canvas. You reach out with both arms, trying to touch something. Anything...

"Look," Jenna says. "There!" Directly before you are two doors, both identical to the one you came in from. Centered between them, slightly higher, is a single window.

"What do we do?" Evan asks.

"We pick one," you say with more confidence than you actually feel. "Before they all disappear."

If you step forward and pick the door on the left, *FLIP ALL THE WAY BACK TO PAGE 15*

Of course, the door to the right looks good also. If you prefer that one, *HEAD TO PAGE 30*

Windows are nice too, I suppose. If you decide to take that route, *TURN TO PAGE 122*

90

"Scotty!"

Jenna's cry comes too late, and from too far away to help. Your right foot plunges through one of the old shelves, causing a cascade of books to tumble down in your direction. You lose your grip on the bookcase, land on your back, and glance up just in time to see the entire six-foot section coming down on you!

As you're buried beneath a few hundred heavy books (not to mention the bookcase itself!) your last thought is to realize this must be

---

THE END

Like it or not, the guy in the painting has two hands. You motion Evan over to help examine it.

"I hate this thing," your cousin says with a shudder. "Whenever I look at it I always feel..."

"Guilty?"

Evan's eyes go wide. "Yes! That's exactly the word!" He regards you suspiciously for a moment. "Guilty."

You set about the grim task of closer examination. The painting itself is very dark – the only non-bright one in the room. Behind the man, off in the distance, is a building or structure. At times it appears to be nothing, but at other times... it looks like the Aurora hotel.

"Is that..."

"Yeah," Evan says. "Maybe."

Against your better judgment, you lean in to get a closer look. Whenever you take your eyes slightly away from it, the whole thing seems to change. Yet when you look at it directly, it morphs back into a shapeless blob. You chalk it up to some sort of peripheral illusion.

"There's nothing behind his hands," Evan says. He pulls the painting from the wall. "And nothing behind the painting either." Your cousin turns the frame around and sets it on the floor, facing downward. He looks highly uncomfortable.

"Okay, what's next?"

Check out the odd metal clock by *GOING TO PAGE 134*
Or examine the painted black vase *OVER ON PAGE 154*

92

Jenna is already halfway to the roof. The snow is coming down even harder now, and conditions are only going to get worse.

"Go," you tell Evan. "I'll be right behind you."

Your cousin hesitates, then nods. He begins his climb, and you stick as close to him as possible. If he falls, there's nothing that will stop him from taking you down with him. But it seems to comfort him just to know that you're there.

"Almost at the top," Jenna calls back. "Keep it up!"

Slowly, carefully, Evan makes his way upward. He's smart enough not to look down. There's a heart-stopping moment when his left hand slips from the facade, but he grabs it again quickly and rights himself.

Finally, you reach the top. Jenna stands over you both, hands on her hips. She looks like a statue in the swirling wind.

"See?" she smiles. "Told ya it was nothing!"

Excellent work (and nice rolling)! Now *TURN TO PAGE 104*

You feel immeasurably better back out in the hallway. The warped sense of distance goes away almost immediately after leaving the room.

Evan taps the manifest. "Next room is 207."

The door to this room opens into frozen darkness. A curtain flaps briskly next to an open window, but the rest of them are drawn tightly against the moonlight. Through the narrow opening you can see snow accumulating out on the fire escape.

"I can't believe the storm's still going," you say. Your cousins don't answer. Behind you, one of them hits the lights.

"Looks pretty plain," Evan says, glancing around. "Except for *that*." He points. Drawn up under the covers, there's a person-sized lump in the center of the bed.

After a moment of indecision you move in, the three of you approaching cautiously from different sides. Nothing resembling a head pokes out from beneath the thick hotel bedspread. Still, you swear you see the rising and falling of someone breathing...

"Is this ghost taking the night off?" Jenna quips, obviously trying to break the tension. "I didn't even know they slept. I mean, why would they need–"

The thing beneath the covers suddenly bolts upright. It throws off the blankets and begins screaming! "W-Who are you?" yells a large, disheveled man. He holds up a thick forearm against the light. "What are you doing in my room!"

"I–I mean we–" Jenna stammers. The man whirls on her, squinting. "Evan!" she shouts. "Why did you–"

"The manifest must be wrong!" Evan cries. "It said this room was unoccupied!"

"Are you trying to rob me?" the man shouts. For someone who just woke up from a dead sleep he sure seems quick to regain his composure. "Not on my watch!"

The three of you turn to run... but the man is too fast. In one fluid motion he leaps from the bed and positions himself between you and the door. "No one's going anywhere!" he roars angrily.

Oops! Bad call! Quick, what should you do?

If you think you can talk your way out of this, try reasoning with the guy *OVER ON PAGE 32*

If you'd rather take your chances out on the snowy fire escape, *FLIP TO PAGE 127*

94

"Well there are a lot more rooms up here," you say, suddenly on the spot. "So maybe I should stick with Evan. We can cover more ground that way."

"Fine," Jenna pouts, pushing her bottom lip out. "Leave me all alone to fend for myself down there." You're about to reconsider when she breaks out laughing. "Just kidding, cuz. Do your thing up here and meet me when you two have finished." She hands her brother the master key and the manifest, then bounces out of the room.

"Alright," you tell Evan. "Where do we begin?"

"Looks like room 102 is unoccupied," he says, studying the piece of paper. "Let's start there."

Silently you slip into the hall. Dim light filters in from antiquated wall fixtures that seem too far apart to be effective. The hotel has an eerie feel to it at this hour. The carpeted hall and papered walls seem to stifle every sound, making you feel that much more claustrophobic.

Evan approaches a door on your right and unlocks it with a muffled *click*. It swings open on silent hinges, revealing a decor that looks strange and alien, yet somehow familiar. It's like stepping back through time.

"This is the 1950's room," Evan says. "One of the Aurora's previous owners thought it would be cool to do theme rooms based on different decades."

Every piece of furniture is styled with a retro-futuristic feel. You see strange, slung back chairs. Stark colors that are bright yet muted. Domed lamps and lacquer-framed artwork are set strategically throughout the room, joined by a star-shaped wall clock that seems to be missing both hands.

A hissing sound seems to be coming from one corner of the room. You approach cautiously, stepping in the direction of the noise.

"It's a phonograph," you say.

"A what?"

"One of those big, antique record players," you tell him. "And for some reason... it's on."

102

TURN OVER TO PAGE 95

There's a record on the turntable, spinning in a hypnotic circle. Without thinking you reach out, grab the playing arm, and set it gently on the vinyl edge.

"What are you doing?" Evan cries. "I don't think–"

Music starts. It's very old and full of brass horns. A woman's voice rises over the melody as she starts singing:

Love is crimson, sometimes gold
Until the blackest lies are told
As thick as ice, all blue and cold
A jealous answer, when unsold

There's a loud pop and the record skips, returning to the beginning. It replays the same song, the same lyrics, then skips back again in an never-ending loop. Eventually you lift up the arm and place it back in its cradle. The player immediately stops spinning.

"Did you turn it off?" Evan asks.

"No."

"Weird." Somehow he's produced a pencil and a tiny, palm-sized notepad.

"What are you doing?" you ask.

Your cousin's hand moves fluidly across the paper. "Writing this down." He doesn't look up. "I write everything down," he shrugs. "It's what I do."

The rest of the room is empty. According to the manifest, you have two choices:

If you decide to enter room 103, *HEAD TO PAGE 56*
If you try your luck with room 105, *TURN TO PAGE 153*

96

As you watch, the darkness within the shattered globe separates. Tendrils of shadow spin outward. Each forms its own distinct thread, twisting through the air as they make their way toward the nethergate. Some rush headlong into it. Others seem to resist, but even those are eventually pulled into the churning void.

When the last of them is gone, you turn back to the table. A second shadow escapes the open book, this one thicker and darker than the rest. This time however, the nethergate's pull is too powerful. With an almost human-like shriek, even this final thread is yanked backward and hurled through the glowing portal.

Everything stops. There's no more wind, no more whispers. A warmth settles over the room, driving away the cold. Your cousins stumble forward, finally released from whatever held them. Jenna is down on one knee. You rush over to help her when she glances over your shoulder and her eyes go wide.

"Look!"

Standing beside James Roakes, right where the mirror-mists were coalescing, is a tall, bearded man. Dressed in a full suit jacket and tie, sporting thick, curling mustaches, there's only one person it can possibly be.

"Alastair!"

The man from the photograph is bent over his great grandson. He slaps him lightly on the cheek a few times, until James's eyes flutter open.

"Wh-what... happened..."

"I'll tell you what happened," Alastair Roakes says, using his actual voice for the first time in over a hundred years. "Your friends here completed my ceremony. They've driven the souls from this place, banished Warrick, and brought me back to the world as well."

You're awestruck. Covered in goosebumps. Your cousins, likewise, are in total shock. James Roakes pulls a flask of water from his pocket and sips from it. He looks up at Alastair and blinks a few times as if seeing a ghost.

Then he springs right out of the chair and bear-hugs him.

"H-how?" is all James Roakes can manage. He says this over a lump in his throat the size of a baseball.

Alastair takes the flask of cold water from his ancestor and takes a long, deep pull. "Ah," he sighs. "Oh, how I've forgotten how good that feels!"

You're still standing there in stunned silence. Ditto for Evan and Jenna. There are a thousand questions you want to ask all at once.

"I suppose you want to know the whole story," Alastair says. He pauses to take the longest, deepest, most satisfying breath anyone has ever taken. He lets it out with a wistful smile. "It was 1909, and the owner of the Aurora hotel had written me a letter. Word of my spiritual abilities had preceded me, and I was invited here to rid this place of lingering souls. When I first arrived here, I was skeptical. Most people who claim to see ghosts are only working themselves up over knocks and shadows."

Alastair stretches his body, staring down at his hands, his arms, his legs. He pats himself as if to make certain he's not dreaming before he continues.

"But no. The Aurora was different. The hotel was haunted not by one spirit, but by many. And they were here well before this place was built. Which meant–"

"Which meant," Evan interrupts, "that the hotel was built over another site!"

Alastair smiles broadly. "Yes. In fact, it was." He gestures to the surrounding chamber. "All of this was here before the Aurora, as the basement of another home. A home owned by a self-proclaimed medium and amateur sorcerer. A man by the name of Warrick Accardis."

"The bad guy," Jenna says. "Right?"

"Yes," Alastair laughs. "Very." He pounds his chest theatrically. "Warrick was a foul man to begin with. He considered himself a magician of sorts, but all he was really doing was dabbling in darkness. Many of the forces he claimed to command were well beyond his control. He died here, trying to open a portal into the spirit world." Alastair points to the wall. "That very portal you all just witnessed."

"And you came here to close it," you say. "This 'nethergate', as you called it."

"Precisely. But I was foolish about one thing..."

98

"You see," Alastair continues, "Warrick perished badly. His body was consumed by his own dark ritual, yet a portion of his enraged spirit still remained. It was trapped there," Alastair points, "within the pages of that book. *His* book."

Jenna's face dawns with realization. "His house was right here," she says. "But once Warrick was gone, they demolished it. Built the hotel over it. Am I right?"

Alastair nods. "Partway through the construction, this sub-basement was discovered. The builder left access to it, intending to use it as a root cellar, for storage. It was here that the book was uncovered."

Evan scratches his head. "But if it was his book," your cousin asks, "why did you include it in your ceremony?"

Your cousin's words are met with a long, silent pause. "That," Alastair sighs, "was my one mistake."

"He came for you, didn't he?" Jenna asks. "And probably when your guard down."

Again Alastair nods. "When Warrick interrupted my ceremony, I thought I was ready for him. I wasn't." The man's words are slower now, laced with bitter memories. "I was too proud. Too arrogant. I allowed him to take hold of me during the ritual, and before I could close the nethergate he pulled me through to the other side!"

James stares at his great grandfather. It occurs to you that physically, Alastair is a good decade younger than him. "H-how are you here right now?" he asks. "Make no mistake," he grins, "I'm thrilled! But... how?"

"I'm here for just one reason," Alastair says. He points to his right hand. "This."

"The ring?" Evan asks. "It saved you?"

"A part of me, yes. But I've also been trapped here since then. Stuck within the confines of the Aurora, unable to leave."

Jenna looks uncomfortable asking her next question. "Do... do you know what year it is?" she asks gently. "Do you know how–"

"How long I've been gone?" Alastair finishes for her. His voice goes low. Melancholy. "Yes, young lady. I've experienced every minute. Been forced to watch the years and decades march by, staring jealously at guests who come and go." He points to the mirror. "It was like looking through glass. I could see everything on the other side in total clarity. Yet I couldn't reach through..."

"Well you're back, now!" you say, trying to be cheerful. "You're here for good, right?"

"Yes," Alastair smiles. "And I have *you* to thank for that." He holds up the ring. "You were wise enough to realize it was the one thing missing."

Jenna's face suddenly lights up. "So it's over? The hotel isn't haunted anymore?"

"No," Evan says. He looks at Alastair slyly. "It's not. And I think I know why."

"Pray tell," Alastair says with a slight bow.

Your cousin points to the table. "That was your crystal globe," Evan says. "You brought it with you. During the ceremony, you planned to gather every last one of the Aurora's spirits within that ball. Then you'd ring the bell and send them back – channeling them through the nethergate before closing it."

Alastair crosses his arms, thoroughly impressed. "Go on."

"So we just finished the ritual," Evan says. "The one you started in 1909. The ring anchored you here while the globe shattered, sending every last restless spirit back through the portal."

"Every one but *you*," Jenna finishes.

James Roakes looks suspiciously back at the book. "Um," he starts carefully. "Warrick included?"

You note a smirk of triumph on Alastair's face. "Yes, even him. His soul was the last to go, and certainly not willingly. The book is nothing now. It's just... a book."

100

"Well," Jenna says, "as far as I'm concerned this leaves only one question left unanswered." Everyone turns to regard her curiously.

"What will you do now?"

James and Alastair glance at each other. They look almost like twins. A lot passes between them, wordlessly.

"Quite honestly," James says, "there's only one thing *to* do."

Alastair finishes the thought for him. "We leave."

Back in the silent world of the hotel lobby, Alastair Roakes looks like he was painted into the architecture itself. From his clothes to his stance to his very presence, he's the epitome of 1900's style – every bit the turn-of-last-century gentleman.

"Are you sure you won't stay here?" Evan asks. "Even for a little while? I'm sure if I talked to my father–"

"No," Alastair smiles. "Thank you, but even the Aurora will agree I've far overstayed my welcome."

James Roakes stands beside his younger great grandfather, which is something you still can't get over. Two very large suitcases rest at his side.

"You're going to have fun," Jenna smiles, tapping Alastair awkwardly on the arm. "Think of all the things you still have to discover! Television, the Internet... riding around in cars..."

"Oh, I've already ridden in automobiles," Alastair says.

Just then a yellow cab pulls up outside. "Not in *that* you haven't," Evan points.

Alastair looks through the window and lets out a nervous chuckle. "What I really desire," he says, "more than anything else, is to travel by airplane."

"Which we will," James adds. "There are a lot of Roakes out there I've lost touch with over the years. And I'm determined to visit them all."

You're left standing there with your cousins, waving through the front doors as the cab pulls slowly away. Its tires spin crazily as it struggles to gain traction. Though the storm has stopped, there's still a good deal of snow on the ground.

Eventually the taillights grow so faint you can no longer see them. The lobby is utterly silent again, except for the occasional sound of Agnes's snoring.

"Well," Jenna says, blowing a bubble. "That was fun."

"And dangerous," Evan adds. "But yeah," he admits. "Fun too."

You stand centered between the twins. "Hotel purged? Evil sorcerer banished?" you cry. "Yeah, I'd say we did alright!" Suddenly and without warning, you throw them both into a playful, simultaneous headlock.

"We saved dad's hotel," Evan says.

"We saved a *life*," Jenna reminds him.

"Hey, the next time you guys need help," you grin, "remind me to–"

"To say no?" Jenna teases.

"No," you laugh. Mid-chuckle, you release a savage yawn. "Next time remind me to get more sleep!"

CONGRATULATIONS!
YOU HAVE REACHED THE ULTIMATE ENDING!

In recognition for your battle against ghosts, spirits, and the possibility of permanent residence at the Aurora, you are hereby granted the title of:

Savior of the Spirit-World!

You may go here: **www.ultimateendingbooks.com/extras.php** and enter code

JR56367

for tons of extras, and to print out your Ultimate Ending Book Five certificate!

And for a special sneak peek of Ultimate Ending Book 6, *JUMP TO PAGE 161*

102

The corridor gives way to the hotel's massive dining hall. At the moment, most of the tables and chairs have been stacked off to the sides, presumably for cleaning. But dead center of the room, seeming to float an inch or so above the ground...

"Whoa," Jenna breathes. "I've never seen *that* before!"

A long, massive table runs down the middle of the hall. High-backed chairs carved with ornate designs sit perfectly arranged, each in its own distinct spot. Still, everything about it seems... off. The color especially, which seems to glow a ghastly blue in comparison to everything else in the dining room. Curiously you find yourself drawn to it. As you do, you pass a tremendous mirror on one wall, also glowing blue.

"*... was good that I wore it...*"

"What?" you say abruptly. You turn to Jenna. "Did you say something?"

"No," she replies distantly. Her eyes are fixed on the table in fascination. "Why?"

"I don't know. I thought I heard–"

"*... had a hand in my own salvation...* "

You start to open your mouth again, but before you can speak something stops you both dead in your tracks. It's a procession. A procession of ghosts! They sweep into the room, men and women dressed in clothing that's unmistakably over a hundred years old. Another ghost floats in to set the table, putting out fancy place settings before each phantom diner. You hear the clatter of silverware. The faint clink of glasses.

"Do you... do you see..."

"YES!" Jenna exclaims. But her look isn't one of horror at all. Your cousin appears thrilled. Exhilarated! She points to the end of the table, where two of the chairs sit completely empty. "Come on!"

You watch uneasily as Jenna slips into one of the open spots at the dining room table. She pats the seat beside her.

"What are you doing?" you hiss. It occurs to you that keeping your voice intentionally low so that 'ghosts' don't hear you is simultaneously hilarious and stupid.

"They want us here," Jenna says plainly. "Look." Sure enough, one of the ghosts across the table seems to be beckoning you over. The thought it can actually *see* you sends a chill down your spine. "See?" Jenna says. "Maybe this is what we're supposed to do."

Gingerly you lower yourself into the last empty seat. Even as you're doing it, you can't even believe it. Another pair of ghosts enters through a wall. They carry platters of glowing blue food. As they circle the table, serving everyone, you can see ghostly steam rising from some of the hot plates. Glasses are filled with a pale amber liquid.

"This is crazy," you whisper to Jenna. Your wide-eyed cousin answers by picking up a fork. You do the same to a spoon, half expecting your hand to pass right though it. It feels cold. Like one of those chilled salad forks you might get at a fancy restaurant.

The ghost who beckoned you over smiles and nods at your food. Spread before you is a bowl of creamy soup, a strange-looking salad, and a thick slice of roast beef. Some of it actually looks quite appetizing.

Okay, here's your bravery test!

If you'd like to try the cream-of-something soup, *HEAD TO PAGE 135*

If you'd rather try the freaky-looking salad, *FLIP ON BACK TO PAGE 65*

If the roast beef looks more appetizing, *TAKE A BITE OVER ON PAGE 152*

If you'd rather just take a sip of the amber liquid, *TURN TO PAGE 55*

Of course, you can also eat nothing. If so, avoid the ghost food and *GO TO PAGE 64*

104

The roof of the Aurora hotel is a beautiful frozen wasteland, lit by the spilled silver light of the almost full moon.

"Wow," Jenna breathes. The steaming fog of her breath is instantly snatched away by the wind. "It's gorgeous up here!"

You're forced to agree. From up here the world takes on an entirely different – and much more serene – perspective. Only Evan, still suffering from his fear of heights, can't appreciate the view.

"You wanna grab my arm?" you offer.

Evan shakes his head. "No, I'm okay. Let's just... go slow."

Moving together, the three of you crunch through the snow. There's ice beneath in some places, making the footing even more treacherous. The smallest slip would send you skidding toward the roof's edge, only to drop you three stories to the ground below.

"W-where do we go f-from here?" you ask, teeth clacking together. The wind at this height is savage, and your T-shirt offers little protection. You think back to the big fireplace you saw in the main lobby. And a cup of hot chocolate has never sounded so good in your life.

"There's a window over there," Jenna says, pointing. Sure enough, a tiny window is set into a mound of snow on the roof. It looks big enough to crawl through.

"Or we could check out the cupola," Evan shouts into the storm. "At the very least it would get us out of this wind, until we decide what to do next."

Well, what's it going to be?
To climb through the strange window set into the snow, *GO TO PAGE 142*
To get out of the snow, and check out the cupola, *TURN TO PAGE 150*

106

You're still not sure which is the right door, but blue has always been your favorite color. Might as well try that one...

"Ready?" you ask Evan, your hand over the knob.

"I guess so," he shrugs. You can tell he's still not totally on board with the whole idea.

"One... two... THREE!"

Your hand clamps down on the doorknob. It takes under a second for you to realize it was the wrong move.

The knob frosts over, fusing your skin to the metal. It's so cold you can't even feel it... until you jerk your hand away and look at the circular black mark on your palm. Your fingers have marks on them too; the dead, blackened tissue of instant frostbite.

"ARGH!!!" Your scream is one of shock – only a reflex, really. That's because you can't even feel the pain yet, although you know the pain is coming.

Evan rushes over as you sink to your knees. With some quick medical attention you'll eventually be able to use your hand again. But for now, this is undoubtedly

THE END

You wince as the shelf beneath your right foot snaps in two! Luckily however, a broken sliver of the wood still holds. You're left dangling by your fingertips... at least until Jenna runs over to support your feet with both hands.

"Climb down," she tells you. "*Slowly.*"

Very carefully you make your way downward. Your cousin guides your ankles until your feet are once again firmly planted on the floor.

"That," Jenna says, "was what you call a bad idea. Next time you should listen to me." She blows a bubble and pops it with her tongue. "Just sayin'."

"Alright," you say begrudgingly. "You're right. You do the top, and I'll do–"

"No need," Jenna says. She smiles as she holds up a large, ancient book with thick metal corner-guards.

"You found it!"

"Yup! And we only had to turn over half the library!" You glance back at the shelves. For the first time, you get a sense of the giant mess you both made.

"Uh, shouldn't we–"

But Jenna is already shaking her head. "Nah. There's no time." She looks around watchfully. "The best thing we can do is get out of here before someone sees us."

Congratulations! You found the book!

Now head into the Aurora's Regency Ballroom by *TURNING TO PAGE 139*

108

You and Evan regroup in the hallway, both glad to be out of that last room. "Things are getting weird," you say, trying to catch your breath.

"Welcome to the Aurora," Evan smirks. "And if you think you've seen weird so far, wait until you've seen this." Your cousin turns and unlocks the door to room 120. It swings wide on creaky hinges, revealing a chamber totally devoid of color. From wall to wall, floor to ceiling, the entire room has been painted black.

"This is getting ridiculous," you say. "Who in their right mind would rent this?"

"Oh you'd be surprised," Evan replies. "Plus, there's some sort of energy to this room. Something that makes people keep coming back. More than any other room in the hotel, this one has the most repeat customers."

You push past your cousin. Shrouded in darkness, the room feels small but somehow not cramped. It's decorated with an eclectic collection of furnishings from a wide range of time periods. All of which have been painted black.

"What's with the artwork?"

The few paintings in the room are the one exception to the rule. Brushed in vibrant colors, they look even brighter than usual against the stygian background. Your cousin shrugs. "I guess they came with the place."

You get to work upending the hotel room. By now you and Evan are experts. Moving quickly and efficiently you find several oddities, but nothing resembling any of the artifacts from Alastair's photograph. You wince at an especially gruesome piece of artwork; a man from the waist up, clutching his chest, his face twisted in pain. Across from him hangs an intricate metal clock that ticks randomly rather than every second.

"The longer I stay here, the creepier this room gets," you say. At that moment, you notice something odd. One of the paintings is hung in a very weird spot, not centered or positioned with the rest of the decor. You unhook it from the wall. Behind it, the black paint is chipped away in a dark, greasy scrawl:

The hands hide the truth

120

You and Evan glance at each other. You have some choices:

To search the ominous painting of the guy clutching his chest, *GO TO PAGE 91*

To examine the strange metal clock, *HEAD TO PAGE 134*

There's also an art-covered vase that's been painted over in black. Search that *WAY DOWN ON PAGE 154*

You place the bell gently back on the table. The second you do, the ball of crystal shatters into a thousand pieces.

The explosion is silent and beautiful. Shards of glimmering, shimmering glass go flying in every conceivable direction. You move one arm up to shield your eyes, but somehow you know it's not necessary. James Roakes, still clutching the wooden table, doesn't even flinch.

A split-second later, it's as if time itself comes to a grinding halt. Everything in the room stops. The wind, the noise, the voices and whispers – these things not only disappear, it's like they were never there to begin with. Your cousins fall forward, having been released from whatever supernatural forces still bound them.

"Mr. Roakes!"

Jenna rushes to the man's aid. You're left standing near the center of the room, ears ringing, arms dangling at your sides.

"It's okay," Jenna says quickly. "He's still breathing."

Together you and Evan help unhook the man's hands from the table. He blinks a few times and raises his chin.

"The crystal..." he says weakly. "Where is it?"

"It's gone," you say. "It exploded."

Mr. Roakes goes limp. It could be exhaustion, it could be relief. Either way it's difficult to tell. Finally he turns his gaze in your direction.

"You rang the bell?" he asks.

"Yes."

You can sense the man's strength returning. He looks back at you now, his steel-grey eyes bearing into your own. Searching your soul...

To your overwhelming relief, he smiles.

A smile... that's a good thing, right? Find out OVER ON PAGE 71

"I think it's that one," you tell Jenna. "The one with the jagged triangle."

Your cousin shifts. One arm goes behind her and deftly slides the old photo from her back pocket. She dangles it downward. "Here. Check."

With a trembling hand you reach up and take it from her. You shift your attention to the photograph for a split second, then quickly back to the task at hand.

"Yeah," you tell her. "That's it!"

Jenna plucks the marked candle from its holder. Then she slides down your back, down the ladder, and holds it steady while you make your way to the floor. You let out the biggest sigh of relief in your entire life. It feels so good you almost want to kiss the ground.

"That was *insane!*" Jenna says, looking back at the ceiling. High above, the candelabra still sways gently from her touch. "I can't believe we *did* that!"

"Me neither," you gasp, hands on your knees. Your voice still shudders. "Come on, let's pack up the ladder and clean this up."

"No time," Jenna says. "Evan's done upstairs. We should go meet him."

"And how do you know that?"

Your cousin's eyes glaze over. She seems to be staring somewhere far away. "It's a twin thing..."

Your eyes narrow. "Really?"

"No silly," Jenna laughs. "He just texted me."

Awesome job! You found the candle!

Head to the hall elevator and meet up with Evan *OVER ON PAGE 157*

You wrack your brain, you scan the room, but you just can't come up with anything beautiful. The feelings of sorrow intensify. Jenna is openly crying.

Suddenly Evan jolts upright. He shakes his head as if clearing it, and the look in your eyes tells you he's back.

"You okay?"

Your cousin lets out a long breath. "Yeah. I think so."

"What can we do for her?" you ask.

"Nothing," Evan replies. "She's stuck here like the rest of them. At least until whatever is wrong with the Aurora gets fixed."

The woman abruptly rises. Still crying, she glides through the room and then fades away.

"Then we *have* to help her," Jenna sniffles, "the only way we can. By fixing this place once and for all."

The rest of the room is empty. There is however, a door to an adjoining suite. Investigate the next room by *TURNING TO PAGE 66*

112

Off to one side of the lobby, a small room seems filled with color. As you step inside, it springs to life as well.

"We call this the Taxidermy room," Jenna says. "All this stuff has been here forever."

Everywhere you look, you see animals. Fish, reptiles, birds – wall to wall, floor to ceiling, the entire area is jam packed. The bust of an elk is mounted high up on one column, alongside an elephant's head that's missing a tusk. You see hawks, owls, sparrows, and some of the ugliest fish you've ever laid eyes on. Some of the creatures are even coming apart. Either they've been neglected or just outlived their extended life spans.

"This is gross," you can't help but say.

"Yeah, dad thinks so too. He says he'll get around to throwing it all away one day, but Evan and I think he's afraid to touch it."

You squint up at one of the mounted heads. "Is that a gryphon?"

Your cousin giggles. "C'mon cuz. Don't get all mythological on me now!"

One deer head in particular catches your eye. Its neck is craned in your direction, its dark glass eyes turned down and lips bared as if snarling at you. It makes you uncomfortable just looking at it.

Jenna appears as disconcerted as you are. "Uh, is that thing *staring* at us?"

You have no answer. It seems silly, but the deer head looks, well... angry.

"Think any of that stuff is here?" you ask. "The bell, book, crystal or candle?" After a cursory examination of the room, your cousin shakes her head. "Good, then let's get out of here. This place is creeping me out."

You really can't get out of the Taxidermy room fast enough.
Head into the Aurora's main hall by *TURNING TO PAGE 133*
Or check out the hotel's dining area by *FLIPPING TO PAGE 102*

114

The book lies open before you, set to a very specific page. *There has to be a reason for that,* you think to yourself.

Leaning in, you look closer. Everything across the pages is gibberish. The series of symbols and strange drawings make no sense at all, yet for some reason you're oddly compelled to stare at them.

Then, all at once, things come into focus. The symbols form words. At times, some of them even make sense. Your lips move unconsciously, without your bidding, and you suddenly find yourself reading...

Mr. Roakes stiffens. His expression is that of a mannequin. In the back of your mind it creeps you out, but you're too busy reading to care. The words flow now, dropping easily from your lips. In a way, you hunger for them. You don't recognize any of the sounds you're making, but each line brings you that much closer to being... sated.

"Scott!" Evan's voice is carried to your ears from somewhere over the wind. He sounds worried. Frantic. But that doesn't matter, because you've already finished. You read through the last symbols on the bottom of the page, and then just as suddenly as it all started, everything stops.

The book slams shut. The candle blows out. The crystal goes back to a simple ball of glass. James Roakes stands straight up, gazes over at you, and smiles. It's not a good smile at all. It's a terrible, hideous grin.

"Thank you," he sneers. He looks down at his hands, his arms, his body. Then he laughs. "Thank you so, so much."

Your mouth goes dry, followed by a terrible sinking feeling in your gut. Looking at Mr. Roakes, an incredible sense of foreboding steals over you.

"Warrick," Evan says from behind you. It's a statement, not a question. "You're Warrick."

The man that used to be Mr. Roakes turns to your cousin, one eyebrow raised in admiration. "Very good," he sneers approvingly. "In fact, excellent. I might even commend you further, if not for the fact that you read my book."

As his gaze goes to the book you take a step backward. Jenna and Evan follow your lead. Mr. Roakes, or Warrick, or whatever he is now, is too busy stretching and regarding his new body. He looks very pleased with himself.

"W– Where's Mr. Roakes?" Jenna stammers.

Warrick smirks. "Which one?"

You take another step while the man stares at his fingers, flexing them.

"You can stop where you are now," he says without looking up. "I'm still going to need you. For a little while, anyway."

You turn and run. Flying past the broken brick corridor you practically hurl yourselves into the elevator. Fortunately the only thing that follows you is laughter. With hands that tremble, you fumble for the key...

Yikes. Not good! Maybe your uncle won't notice you've unleashed a raving sorcerer on his century-old hotel. In any case, this is totally

THE END

116

The door to the closet is open. The janitor's not there. Getting his keyring would quick. Easy.

"Maybe we should just swipe the key," you say, agreeing with Evan. "Hurry, let's do it."

Silently the three of you slip into the janitor's closet. The scent of bleach and cleaning products is almost overpowering.

"There!" Evan indicates. "The keyring is right there on the pegboard."

KA-CLACK!

You spin around as the door closes behind you. To your surprise there's now a rolled-up extension cord on the floor. It's the last thing you see before the lights go out. "Wait! What just happened?"

"He's leaving!" Jenna hisses. Sure enough you hear footsteps padding along the hallway carpet. They grow fainter with every step. "We're locked in!"

"Calm down," you say. "It's no big deal. We'll just unlock the door from the insid–"

The words die in your throat as your hand finds the doorknob. It's cold. Smooth. Featureless.

"There's no way to unlock it from this side," Jenna laments. "We're stuck here until he comes back."

"Which is when?"

"Tomorrow afternoon," Evan sighs dejectedly. "Or wait... isn't Vincent off on Sundays?"

Well, I guess that's it. You got far, but not far enough. Hey, maybe you could bang on the door loud enough for someone to hear you. Then again, the only one up right now is Agnes. And she's nearly deaf...

Oh well. Looks like you've reached

THE END

The Aurora's kitchen is filled with a mismatch of modern and outdated. Stainless steel racks rest beside sixty-year old wooden counter tops. An original ceramic oven is flanked neatly by two cutting edge gas burners.

Steam rises from several large pots fed by intense blue flame. You peek over the edge to find them at a rolling boil. "Are they cooking at this hour?" you ask.

Jenna steps out of a small walk-in, casually munching on something she swiped. "No," she says in answer to your question. "But Marco likes to sterilize everything at night. He boils *everything*. It's kinda weird, but–"

The sound of someone approaching cuts her off. Your cousin pushes you backward, to where an over-sized dish machine is crammed into too small an area.

"This was a mistake," she whispers. "With all the cleaning and prep-work, the kitchen is too busy. Even at night."

A man who you can only assume is Marco walks past you. He has the quick stride of someone always in a hurry. Behind him you hear more noise, more people heading your way.

"We need to get out of here," Jenna says. "Fast!"

You need to move quickly! Roll a single die.

If you rolled a 1, *HEAD TO PAGE 83*

If you rolled a 2, 3, 4, or 5, *TURN TO PAGE 155*

If you rolled a 6, *FLIP BACK TO PAGE 19*

118

Gathering all your strength, you give one last push against your invisible attacker. At the same time, you scream your throat raw at the top of your lungs!

There's a loud *boom* – like a small clap of thunder – that comes from somewhere above you. Then, all at once, the weight is gone. A rush of wind tears through the room as you suck great gobs of air into your battered lungs. You can breathe again!

Off to your side, Evan is slowly getting to his feet. He looks like he's been through all twelve rounds of a boxing match.

"Let's get out of here," he gasps, his voice hoarse and broken. "Now."

Nice job, you fought your way free! Now slip across the hall by *TURNING TO PAGE 138*

"Wait here!" you say. "I'll be right back!"

It takes forever to reach the door of this crazy room. When you finally do, you slip back into the hall and silently backtrack to where you saw the other elephant tusk. The halls of the Aurora are thankfully empty, and you encounter no one else along the way.

Minutes later you re-enter room 202, dragging a three-foot long piece of pointed ivory behind you. Evan and Jenna are staring at you like you have three heads.

"I knew I saw this somewhere," you say. Hefting it onto your shoulder, you slide the tusk snugly into the elephant statue. It matches the other one perfectly.

"Look!" Jenna says.

As you release your grip on the tusk, the elephant's mouth grinds open. An object drops out, glimmering brightly as it lands at your feet. You pick it up.

"It's a ring."

"A girl's ring?" Jenna asks hopefully.

"No," you say. "I don't think so. Too big."

The ring is a thick band of gold topped by a large, multi-faceted stone. Deep within it you can make out a muddy, reddish glow. It looks old. Evan takes it from you and examines it thoroughly before giving it back.

"Cool ring I guess," he shrugs. "But let's keep moving. We're not going to find anything here, and this place is making me dizzy."

Head back into the hallway by *TURNING TO PAGE 93*

120

You jolt forward, throwing your arm out, reaching for the marked candle... but you miss! Helplessly you watch as it slams to the floor and breaks in half!

"Oh no!"

A bunch of other candles rain down on you. Some of them bounce off your back. Others thud loudly against the polished oaken floor.

Jenna looks crestfallen. "What are we going to do now?" She picks up the broken candle, her expression miserable. "Maybe we could–"

"I'll tell you what you're going to do now," a stern voice calls from behind you. You wince as you recognize your Uncle Gus. "First, you're going to clean up this mess. And right after that, you're both going back to your rooms!"

Oops! Busted!

Well, the night didn't pan out quite the way you wanted it to. If only you'd been quicker! Sorry to say though, for now this looks like

THE END

You wind back and punch through the glass window of the cupola. There's no noise at all as the already cracked pane gives way easily.

"Are you alright?" Evan asks quickly.

A bit apprehensively you unwrap your arm and check for injury. Nothing!

Evan takes back his sweatshirt while Jenna steps up to examine your handiwork. The hole you made in the glass is very small. Luckily, it's close enough to the door that Jenna can reach right in and unlock it.

"Get inside!" she urges. "I want to close this door as quickly as possible!"

Nice work!

Get into the cupola and out of the wind *WHEN YOU TURN TO PAGE 88*

122

Left... right... you decide to split the difference. "We're taking the window," you tell your cousins. "Before this room gets any weirder."

"Is that even possible?" Jenna asks, laughing.

"Probably not. But I'm not sticking around to find out." With your cousins close behind, you throw open the window. A blast of cold air and blowing snow hits you square in the face. "It leads outside," you call back. "There's some kind of a ledge here."

Evan moves beside you to investigate. "Yeah, this is part of the stone facade. It runs around the entire hotel."

Behind you, the room appears to be spinning. It also looks as if the walls are closing in. Jenna pushes past you and climbs out onto the ledge. She looks totally comfortable, even in the raging snowstorm. "Come on," she urges. "We can climb up to the roof from here."

Evan's expression tells a much different story. Unlike his sister he's absolutely frozen with terror.

"Forget about your fear of heights," you implore him. You jerk your thumb back toward the room, which now appears as a chaotic swirl of light and dark. "This is the only way."

Thankfully, this motivates him. A minute later the three of you are pressed tightly against the stone ledge of the Aurora's rear wall.

"We have to climb up!" Jenna yells over the wind. She's pointing. You can see a number of decorative stones that would make fine handholds, although they look more than a little icy. "It's easy," Jenna adds. "I've done it before."

"That was in the summer!" Evan shouts back. He shoots you a grim look. You can tell the climb is going to be hard for him.

You reach for one of the handholds. As you do, you notice several depressions set at even intervals leading up toward the roof. Almost like a reverse ladder. An inscription runs along the apron of the ledge, except for one spot where there's a square-shaped hole. It looks like something fits into it. Something that would have writing on one side.

Do you have something that fits into the square hole? If so, add the letters of that word together using the chart below, and then *GO TO THAT PAGE*

A = 1	F = 6	K = 11	P = 16	U = 21	Z = 26
B = 2	G = 7	L = 12	Q = 17	V = 22	Example:
C = 3	H = 8	M = 13	R = 18	W = 23	ANNA =
D = 4	I = 9	N = 14	S = 19	X = 24	1+14+14+1
E = 5	J = 10	O = 15	T = 20	Y = 25	= 30

If you don't have anything that fits, it's time to climb!

Roll two dice (or just pick a random number from 2 to 12)

If the sum of your roll comes up an EVEN number, *HEAD TO PAGE 78*

If the two dice add up to an ODD number instead, *GO TO PAGE 92*

124

"Come with me," Jenna tells you over the noise. "I know what to do."

Your cousin takes your hand and pulls you down the right-side corridor. The two of you hug the wall for a moment as a man approaches from the left. It's Uncle Gus! Thankfully he turns without noticing you, walking back the way you came.

"That was close," you breathe. When you look back, Jenna's already moved further down the hall toward the source of the noise. A thin, older man is shampooing the rug with a giant silver machine.

"Jenna!" you cry out in warning. Your voice comes off as more of a strangled whisper. But it's too late – the man has already seen her. His reaction however, is not what you expect. He looks up at her and smiles. Then he flips a switch, and the machine powers down with a long, winding *whir.*

"Scotty," Jenna says, "this is Vincent. He's been the janitor here for a really long time."

The man extends a calloused hand and you take it. His grip is warm and strong. "Pleased to meet you, Scotty."

"Uh, yeah," you smile awkwardly. "Nice to meet you too." Vincent looks like the epitome of every janitor you've ever seen, right down to the big ring of keys at his hip. You notice that one of them – a long silver one with teeth on both sides – seems different from the others.

Jenna is looking down at the rug. Vincent follows her gaze, scratching his head. "Same spot?" she asks.

"Yup," the janitor laments. "Every night I clean it. And every morning it's back, same spot, same size and shape." You can make out a dark stain on the rug now. It looks reddish-brown, like the color of rust... or something worse. "No matter what I do, it keeps rising up," Vincent says. "But your dad wants it clean, so..."

"What do you think it is?" you find yourself asking.

The janitor shrugs. "Dunno. But something happened here, a long time ago." The man looks over his shoulder warily. "And whatever it was," he says, his voice now suddenly low, "the Aurora *remembers.*"

"Tell him about the ghosts!" your cousin chimes in.

Vincent looks uncomfortable. His eyes shift left to right. "Now Jenna, you know your father doesn't want me talking about–" Her intense look of disappointment stops him. "Oh all right. Yes," he says in an even more conspiratorial tone. "This place is haunted. On this night especially, above all others." The janitor suppresses a shudder. "You should be careful around here. You'd be safer in your rooms. In fact, what are you doing–"

"Up at this hour?" Jenna finishes. "We're looking for... a few things."

"What kind of things?"

"An very old book. A bell. A candle. A crystal ball."

Vincent's eyes narrow. You can't believe Jenna is telling him all this! Still, the man doesn't bat an eyelash. He taps one finger on his chin before speaking again.

"For the book, you could check the lounge," the janitor says. "It used to be the old hotel library."

"Good idea!" Jenna says. "Thanks Vincent!"

"As for the candle... I don't know. This place is old. There are bound to be a lot of candles." Vincent pauses for a moment, as if considering something. "And one more thing," he says, his voice going low. "Beware of Warrick."

"Warrick?"

You can tell by the way the man winces that Jenna uttered the word too loudly for his tastes. "Yes, him. Of all the spirits here, he's... the bad one."

Your cousin starts to say something else but the sound of more footsteps rises from the hall. Vincent looks worried. "Got to get back to work," he says, kicking on the shampoo machine. He winks at Jenna. "Good luck you two!" he shouts over the noise. "And be *careful*."

You can no longer hear the footsteps over the whirring of the machine, so you'll need to move quickly:

A large exit behind you leads to the hotel lounge. Check that out *OVER ON PAGE 49*

Also, you notice the janitor's closet is open. Investigate it by *GOING TO PAGE 23*

126

After consulting the manifest, you enter room 121. Immediately you're forced to shield your eyes, because with the moonlight streaming in through the windows everything is impossibly bright.

"A white room?" you ask. "How the heck does your father keep this one clean?"

The walls, floor, ceiling, bed, furniture... everything here is painted a stark, immaculate white. Everything, that is, except five narrow doors on one wall. The doors themselves are washed in bright, primary colors. Left to right, they are red, blue, green, black, and gold.

"What are these all about?" you ask Evan. But your cousin isn't answering. He's just staring at the doors in disbelief.

"Dunno," he breathes. "They've never been here before."

The doors stand out in stark contrast to the rest of the pure white room. Each sports a single knob, with no lock or keyhole.

"Which one do we open?" you ask.

Evan looks at you like you just suggested walking across hot coals. "None of them?" he suggests. "They're not part of the hotel, I don't think. They can't lead anywhere good..."

"C'mon," you say. "Your sister would've had three of these doors open by now. We couldn't stop her if we wanted to. And you're saying you're not even curious? Are you *really* her twin?" Evan's eyebrows knit together in what might be indignation. It's hard to tell. "Come on," you urge again. "After all, we *are* searching for things here."

Your cousin still looks apprehensive. "Okay," he says finally, "let's try one." He pauses, biting his lip. "But have we gotten any hints so far as to which one to go with?"

121

Alright, it's time to pick a door! But choose wisely...

If you decide to open the *RED* door, *TURN TO PAGE 22*

If you decide to open the *BLUE* door, *TURN TO PAGE 106*

If you decide to open the *GREEN* door, *TURN TO PAGE 136*

If you decide to open the *BLACK* door, *TURN TO PAGE 36*

If you decide to open the *GOLD* door, *TURN TO PAGE 145*

"Fire escape!" you yell to your cousins. "Now!"

Jenna doesn't need to be told twice. She bolts past you and scrambles onto the snow-covered ledge. Evan moves less decisively, but you usher him through quickly and slam the window shut behind you.

"Get back here!" the man shouts. His threat is muffled by the storm and thick glass.

You whirl, confused to see both your cousins climbing up instead of down. They continue along the fire escapes' metal ladder until they're standing on the roof.

"Come on!" Jenna shouts back. Her brother, standing next to her, looks utterly mortified. A memory floats back to you – something about your cousin Evan and a debilitating fear of heights.

There's nothing else to do but climb. You grit your teeth against the cold, fingers clinging painfully to the frozen rungs as you push your way upward and into the swirling snow. It's not long before you've reached the end. Standing next to your cousins on the roof of the Aurora hotel, you peer three long stories straight down.

"Tell me again why I agreed to come here?" you say, teeth chattering.

"Because you love us!" Jenna shouts, wrapping her arms around you.

I'd say things are heating up, but that would be an outright lie.
Bundle up and *TURN TO PAGE 104*

128

Riding a squeaky glass elevator straight into the lobby doesn't seem like a good way to stay low profile. "Let's take the stairs," you tell Jenna.

The Grand Staircase is a wood-paneled masterpiece. You follow your cousin down each carpeted step, clutching a banister worn smooth by a centuries' worth of visitors. Halfway down, a strange feeling steals over you. You have the distinct sensation of being watched, but when you turn around of course nothing is there.

"You get it too, huh?" Jenna calls from over her shoulder. "We all do. It's no biggie."

A statue stands at the base of the staircase, perched tall on the last baluster. The sculpture is of a strikingly beautiful woman with a mouthful of broken teeth. You can't tell if her teeth were broken later on, of if they were part of the original artwork.

"I dare you," Jenna says.

"To what?"

"To put your finger in her mouth!" Your cousin waits for your reaction before smiling mischievously. "It's said to be good luck if she doesn't bite you."

"And what if she *does* bite me?"

Jenna laughs. "Try it and find out."

If you stick your finger in the statue's mouth, *HEAD BACK TO PAGE 53*

What are you, *crazy?* Skip the whole thing and go to the lobby by *TURNING TO PAGE 68*

"Don't fight it!" you shout. The words come out strange because you can't even unclench your jaw. "We can't... try... to..."

Clearing your mind, you force yourself to relax. You let your thoughts go clear, your body limp. The pressure eases, ever so slightly. You relax further, and it lets up even more.

Slowly you allow yourself sit up. The hum in the air is gone. Although your body still tingles, you're no longer gripped by whatever was pushing down on you. You stand, flexing your hands and fingers tentatively.

At last, Evan stirs. You reach down and help him to his feet.

"How did you know?" you cousin asks. His whole body is still shaking. "Not to fight it, I mean. How could you be so sure it would let go of us?"

"I wasn't really," you admit. "But I heard a voice..." You turn to face the mirror. The only thing looking back at you is your own reflection. "Or at least, I *thought* I did."

Evan lets out a shuddering sigh. "No," he says, "I'm sure you did. And it wouldn't be the first time Jenna or I heard stuff like that around here." He checks himself from head to toe, then claps you on the shoulder. "Thanks though. Now let's get out of here before that...*thing* comes back."

Cross the hall and search room 106 by *TURNING TO PAGE 138*

130

The vase is dark and (potentially) full of terrors. You're not sticking your arm in there.

"Help me lift it," you say to Evan. "Gently."

Together you hoist the vase into the air. Even the bottom is painted black. You upend it over the bed, just in case anything fragile is inside...

"Watch out!"

Evan springs back as a giant centipede crawls out of the vase! You nearly drop it as the creature slithers across the jet black bedspread. It disappears somewhere behind the headboard.

"Sorry," Evan says sheepishly. Rightfully embarrassed, he helps you lower the vase back to the floor. He uses his cell phone's flashlight to check the interior. There's nothing else.

You nod at his makeshift flashlight. "That's a good idea," you say. "Why didn't you think of it before?"

Your cousin shrugs. "Just thought of it now."

Whew! You dodged an insect there! (or more accurately an arthropod)

Check out the strange metal clock *OVER ON PAGE 134*

"I'll do the upper shelves," you tell your cousin. "It looks a little dicey and I don't want you getting hurt."

Jenna starts to pout, but then stops herself. "Awww, that's sweet! Fine Scotty. You do the top."

The two of you make fast work of the library. The midnight silence is broken by the constant *thump thump thump* of books being turned on their spines. Every once in a while you step on a shelf that feels springy, causing you to be careful with how you distribute your weight.

Halfway through, you still haven't found a single book with corner-guards. You're starting to get discouraged when suddenly–

SNAP!

One of the shelves gives way beneath you!

Quick, roll two dice! (Or just roll the same die twice)

If the total of your roll is an ODD number, *HEAD TO PAGE 90*

If the total of your roll is an EVEN number, *FLIP BACK TO PAGE 107*

132

You drop to your knees and start rolling back the rug. It's easy work, and soon you've exposed most of the floor directly under the painting.

"There," Evan says abruptly. "Look at that."

A trio of symbols have been painstakingly carved into the floor. The middle one is crudely circled in red... in what you really, really hope not to be blood.

"Two doors," you wonder aloud. "And that looks like a window. Any ideas?" you ask your cousin.

Evan's notepad is out. Already he's drawn a crude sketch of the floor. "Nope. None at all."

You roll the rug back over the carvings. "Alrighty then," you say, standing up so fast your knees pop. "Let's keep this ball rolling."

The fun continues *OVER ON PAGE 35*

You enter the hotel's main hall. A plush carpet stretches its entire length, embroidered with designs that are very old yet very cool. You follow the wide corridor until it comes to a T-shaped intersection.

"What's that noise?"

Somewhere off to your right, the steady whining sound of a large machine breaks the silence. At the same time, you can hear heavy footsteps coming in from the left. And they're getting louder. Closer...

Jenna grabs your arm. "Quick!" she says. "We can't be caught down here!"

Hurry! Flip two coins (or just flip the same coin twice):

If both coins come up *HEADS, TURN TO PAGE 21*

If both coins come up *TAILS, HEAD ON DOWN TO PAGE 67*

If the coins come up with one of each, *GO TO PAGE 124*

134

You scan the room one final time. Then you smile. "I've got it!"

"Got what?"

"The answer to our riddle," you tell your cousin. He still looks confused.

"There was a riddle?"

You glare at him dubiously. It's times like these when you wonder if you're truly related. "Yeah, man," you say. "Think about it. Aside from you and I, what in this room has hands?"

Evan has to follow your gaze before it finally dawns on him. "Oh yeah! The clock!"

Together you approach the strange metal clock. As you pull it from the wall, it's every bit as heavy as you imagine it to be.

"There's nothing behind it," Evan says.

You pull a small multi-tool from your back pocket in answer. Settling on a screwdriver, you carefully remove the clock's back panel. Even the gears and sprockets inside the clock have been painted!

"Now *that's* dedication," Evan exclaims.

"No cousin," you tell him. "That's just weird." You continue removing pieces of the clock and setting them aside haphazardly. It's obvious you have no intention of ever putting the thing back together. Finally, deep inside, you see a glimmer of steel. Or what looks to be steel...

"It's the bell!"

A few pieces later you pull out a small silver bell. It looks exactly like the bell in Alastair's photograph.

"No wonder this clock never worked right," Evan swears.

Congratulations! You found the silver bell!

Head back into the hallway when you *FLIP TO PAGE 14*

You're already holding the spoon so you dip into the soup. You blow on it – pausing only to think of how absurd that is – then bring it to your lips.

It's creamy and full of mushrooms. Tasty, even. Despite not really being hungry you find yourself going back for more. You're halfway through the bowl, in fact, when you realize Jenna is staring at you.

"Cuz?"

You look back at her curiously. All of a sudden everything seems weird. Out of focus.

"You okay?" she asks.

"Yeah fine," you say. But you're not fine. Not really. The spoon is no longer in your hand and you feel woozy and weird. You're about to tell this to Jenna when...

You wake up in an ambulance! Evan and Jenna are hunched over you, looking extremely worried. Somewhere behind one of the paramedics is your Uncle Gus, sitting with his head in his hands.

"Wh– what happened?"

"Jenna tells me you ate some mushroom soup," Evan says. You nod glumly. "Served to you by ghosts," your cousin continues.

You wince, your heart sinking as you realize the foolishness of the whole idea. What in the world were you thinking? Something turns over unpleasantly in your stomach. Jenna catches your gaze, looking absolutely miserable. She shrugs back at you apologetically.

Well, on one hand you'll probably be okay. And you got to try ghost-soup! On the other however, is the nagging reminder that this is unfortunately

THE END

136

You stop to think for a moment. Then something occurs to you. "Remember that song on the phonograph?" you say. "Wasn't it about colors?"

Evan pulls out his notepad and flips to a page. "Yeah, actually you're right. It had all these colors, and–"

"And the last line," you say. "What was it?"

Evan glances down and reads it to you: "*A jealous answer, when unsold.*"

You smile triumphantly. "That's it!"

"What's it?"

"The right answer," you say. "Jealousy is green. We should pick the green door!"

Your cousin's eyes narrow as he regards you skeptically. "Yeah, right."

In answer you step forward and pull open the green door. Beyond it is a small rectangle of black space. The space shimmers and wavers, almost as if it's not a part of the room at all. It looks... well, fake. The words 'extra-dimensional' come to mind.

In the center of the space floats a large crystal ball.

"That's it!" Evan cries. You're so busy gloating you haven't even moved. "Hurry up! Grab it!"

Less than enthusiastically you reach out beyond the door, waiting for something bad to happen. Nothing does. You grab the ball, which feels smooth and cool and perfectly normal. You pull it out and kick the door closed with your toe.

"We got it!" Evan shouts. "We got one of the artifacts!"

"Ahem," you grunt, clearing your throat. "*We?*"

Congratulations, you recovered the crystal ball! What's next?

The room next door seems to have no number. You can check it out *OVER ON PAGE 38*

Or you can cross the hall and search room 116. To do that, *GO TO PAGE 62*

The three of you hurry to the elevator. Evan thumbs the 'B' button, and the doors open into the basement. Almost immediately you encounter a locked door. Evan produces the master key, and moments later you're walking through a large warehouse of hotel-related items. There are stacks and shelves everywhere, containing everything from toilet paper and cleaning products to soap, pillows and linens.

"This place is clean," you say. "Too new and modern. Do you have any idea where Alastair would've held his ceremony?"

Jenna casts Evan a concerned look. "That's just it, cuz. We really don't."

Evan nods. "Yeah, we've been down here a bunch of times. Moved stuff around, swept all the floors, even the walls. If there was an explosion down here, someone did an awesome job cleaning it up."

You fan out, checking for evidence of anything out of the ordinary. You even consult Alastair's photo, but to avail. Nothing is recognizable, and the place is just too well-kept. It doesn't look anything like you'd expect from a hundred year old basement. Unless...

"Come on!" you say. "I think I know where we need to be!" Evan and Jenna follow you eagerly, at least until you lead them back into the elevator. Then they look confused.

"Scotty, what–"

"*This,*" you say, pointing beneath the elevator's modernized electronic panel. A small, silver-colored keyhole is recessed into the wood. "I noticed it earlier. It must be from when the hotel was first built." You glance up at your cousins. "Do you have the key for that?"

If you already know who has the silver key, add the letters in that word together using the chart below and then *GO TO THAT PAGE*

A = 1	F = 6	K = 11	P = 16	U = 21	Z = 26
B = 2	G = 7	L = 12	Q = 17	V = 22	Example:
C = 3	H = 8	M = 13	R = 18	W = 23	ANNA =
D = 4	I = 9	N = 14	S = 19	X = 24	1+14+14+1
E = 5	J = 10	O = 15	T = 20	Y = 25	= 30

If you're not sure where to get the key, *TURN TO PAGE 26*

138

You cross through the threshold of room 106. Orange and brown furniture clashes with horrible floral print wallpaper. They both do battle with a set of thick, paisley curtains.

"This is the 1960's room, isn't it?" you ask.

Evan responds with a chuckle. "You're catching on quickly."

A giant dinosaur of a TV set sits like a pile of cinder blocks against one wall. Two long metal antennae stick up from the top in a 'V' pattern.

"Is that thing black and white?" you ask. Before Evan can answer, the television clicks on. Beneath the angry buzz of white noise a picture fades slowly into view. But there's no reception. Nothing but 'snow'.

"*Finish it!*"

The voice is crisp, loud, staccato. It blurts forth from the TV's internal speaker. Evan is looking at you, presumably for an answer. "Finish what?" your cousin asks. "What do you think that–"

"*The page...*" the voice rasps. "*Finish the–*"

The air behind you comes to life with a huge burst of static. You whip around to find a box-shaped transistor radio has turned on. The dial on the radio is spinning on its own, flipping wildly through the channels.

"*Don't,*" the radio tells you. "*Don't... can't... should not...*"

The noise in the room grows louder as the TV and radio compete with one another. In the meantime, the air crackles with an almost electrical charge. You smell something burning, like ozone. Glancing down, the hairs on your arms are standing right on end.

"*NO!*" You can't tell if the word comes from in front or behind. A blast of energy strikes you like a physical blow, and then suddenly you and Evan are being shoved through the door and out into the hall. The door slams violently shut behind you.

Evan appears shaken. "But we didn't even get to finish the room," he says forlornly.

"I'm pretty sure," you tell him, "that room is finished with *us*."

Wanna try room 108? *HEAD TO PAGE 41*

How about room 109? *TURN TO PAGE 47*

The majestic beauty of the Regency Ballroom lays stretched out before you. It's easy to know, after just a single glance, that this room was most likely the heart and soul of the Aurora hotel.

"There!" Jenna exclaims. She points upward, to where an ancient iron candelabra dangles from the ceiling. Loaded within, you see a circle of time-yellowed candles. "It's got to be one of those," Jenna says. "They've been here forever and no one ever lights them."

You squint upward. The candles certainly *look* right, at least from here. If only they were a little closer so you could get a better view of them...

"How do you think we should–" Halfway through your sentence you realize Jenna is gone. You're left standing in the ballroom alone, when all of a sudden–

Screeeeeech!

Your cousin re-enters the room dragging a large rickety-looking step-ladder. You rush over to help her out, mostly to put an end to the horrendous noise. "Where'd you get *this*?" you ask incredulously.

"From the janitor's closet."

You blink in disbelief. "Well then why didn't we use it in the library!"

Jenna blows a bubble and shrugs. "Just remembered it."

You consider the ladder for a moment, then glance back to the ceiling. "Well we can't use it anyway," you tell her. "It's not going to reach."

"If I stand on your shoulders it will."

Your stomach lurches. You're not a fan of heights to begin with, but the thought of your cousin climbing over you while standing atop that ladder is enough to make you physically ill. "Is there any other way?" you ask nervously.

Jenna bites her lip, lost in thought. "Yeah maybe." She fishes into her pocket and pulls out a long piece of string. Then, grabbing the small bronze sculpture of a bird from a nearby table, she begins wrapping one end of the string around it. You look on, impressed.

"What else have you got in your pockets?"

Your cousin laughs. "Wouldn't *you* like to know."

Will you try slinging a bird sculpture at the chandelier to knock down the candles? *GO TO PAGE 34*

Or would you rather stack two people at the top of a very tall ladder? If so *TURN TO PAGE 74*

140

You approach the door to room 202. As you do, you realize the number plate has been screwed on upside down.

"Looks more like 505," Jenna notes.

"Or SOS," Evan says.

Considering the stuff you've seen at the Aurora so far, that last thought is more than a little disquieting. Evan unlocks the door. It sticks at first, then swings open into a small room filled with an impossibly large amount of stuff.

Everything here is weird and mismatched. The jumble of furnishings, decor, and random objects scattered throughout the room make absolutely not sense. In fact, the room itself feels totally off.

"It can't be this big," Jenna says. You know exactly what she means. The tiny room feels like it expanded since you entered, as if it somehow grew in size. It looks like someone dumped the entire contents of their attic in here. Everything seems either too big or too small for the room, without exception.

Nervously you glance back at the door, which now seems tiny and very far away. You've only taken three or four steps inside, you realize. The place reminds you of staring into a giant fun-house mirror.

"Start searching through all this stuff I guess," Evan mutters. Though he's standing right next to you, his voice seems like he's calling to you from off in the distance.

The three of you get to work sweeping the hotel room. Evan checks about a dozen pieces of random furniture. Jenna upends an array of dusty boxes, only to find more boxes inside. You search through a series of trunks and crates, only to turn around and find a brand new stack of identical trunks and crates standing behind you. "Something's up," you say finally. "I think we're wasting our time here."

That's when you notice the elephant statue. It's very large and beautiful, except that it's missing a tusk.

If you know which room the other tusk is in, *TURN TO THAT ROOM'S NUMBER*. Or if that room is a word, add the letters of the word together using the chart below and then *GO TO THAT PAGE*.

A = 1	F = 6	K = 11	P = 16	U = 21	Z = 26
B = 2	G = 7	L = 12	Q = 17	V = 22	Example:
C = 3	H = 8	M = 13	R = 18	W = 23	ANNA =
D = 4	I = 9	N = 14	S = 19	X = 24	1+14+14+1
E = 5	J = 10	O = 15	T = 20	Y = 25	= 30

If you can't locate another elephant tusk, that's okay. Head to the next room *OVER ON PAGE 93*

142

You enter the coldest and oldest room yet. Moonlight filters in through the small, open window off to one side.

"I know what this is!" Evan cries. "This is one of those little gables that sticks out of the roof!" He punches his sister lightly in the arm. "You know what I mean – those little decorative things that stick out on top, with the tiny windows."

Jenna's expression is one of realization. "Oh yeah!" she exclaims. "There are a bunch of them, I think. But didn't dad say they were only for decoration?"

"Not this one apparently," Evan shrugs. You can tell this room has been sealed off for a very long time. The furnishings and fixtures are ancient, most of the wood cracked or splintered from the cold. It looks like the perfect place to find something important. If only you knew what you were looking for!

"Check it out, a trunk!" Jenna says excitedly. She flips it open. "Awww, it's empty."

An even frostier blast of cold washes over you. Every muscle in your body tenses up as you feel that all-too familiar tingling sensation.

"There," Evan whispers. "Look!"

In the corner of the room, the apparition of a young man is hunched over a low table. He sits in contemplation for several moments, two fingers on his chin. Eventually he rises and walks the length of the room, never taking his eyes from the table. Then he returns to his original position.

"What's he doing?"

You creep closer. There's a chessboard on the table, arranged mid-game. The pieces are old and dark – probably cast from pewter, as far as you can tell. The young ghost keeps pacing the room along the same path, returning again and again to contemplate the board on some kind of bizarre, endless loop.

Evan examines the board, his lips moving silently. "I only count 31," he says, "including those that were captured." He looks up at you. "That means there's a piece missing."

Do you have the missing chess-piece? If so, what is it? Add up the all the letters in that word using the chart below, then *TURN TO THAT PAGE*

A = 1	F = 6	K = 11	P = 16	U = 21	Z = 26
B = 2	G = 7	L = 12	Q = 17	V = 22	Example:
C = 3	H = 8	M = 13	R = 18	W = 23	ANNA =
D = 4	I = 9	N = 14	S = 19	X = 24	1+14+14+1
E = 5	J = 10	O = 15	T = 20	Y = 25	= 30

If you don't have the chess-piece, that's okay. Exit through the window and cross the frozen rooftop *OVER ON PAGE 150*

144

The crystal globe swirls with darkness. The candle flickers. But the silver bell, you notice, sits on the table very unassumingly.

On a whim, you reach out and ring it.

Your glance back at the table just as the book slams shut. The candle goes out. Yet the ball of crystal, resting in its cradle, is still spinning with an inner darkness. It's moving even more wildly now, as if feeding off the light in the room – or maybe the energy of the nethergate itself.

Something behind Mr. Roakes catches your eye. A glint in the mirror, or maybe a trick of the eye. For a brief moment, it looks like a figure. A man perhaps, standing there in the shadowy world behind the glass.

...must not all be here. Something else...

You follow the mirror-man's gaze downward to where James Roakes is still seated at the table. His body is convulsing all over. His hands clutch the edge of the table like iron claws.

Do you have anything else to add to the ceremony? Some last second addition?

If so, take the *four* letters in that word and add them together, using the chart below. Once you have the total you can *GO TO THAT PAGE*

A = 1	F = 6	K = 11	P = 16	U = 21	Z = 26
B = 2	G = 7	L = 12	Q = 17	V = 22	Example:
C = 3	H = 8	M = 13	R = 18	W = 23	ANNA =
D = 4	I = 9	N = 14	S = 19	X = 24	1+14+14+1
E = 5	J = 10	O = 15	T = 20	Y = 25	= 30

If you don't know what else to do right now, that's fine. See what happens next when you *TURN TO PAGE 109*

The gold door shimmers in the filtered moonlight. It actually looks inviting.

"Here goes nothing," you tell Evan.

Your hand closes over the knob. It feels warm. Satisfying. You stand there for a moment just enjoying it, noting that the sensation seems to travel upward and throughout your entire body. It feels like you just sank into a hot tub on a really cold night.

"Well?" Evan says. "You gonna open it?"

"Yeah," you say distantly. "In a minute." With embarrassment you realize that you're actually smiling. "Okay sure, I guess so."

You open the door. There's nothing behind it. All you see is more of the pure white wall.

"Guess that's not it," Evan says. "Or maybe all these doors lead to nothing. If so, we're wasting our time."

The warmth is still with you as you close the door. You do it slowly, savoring the body-engulfing feeling of pure euphoria.

"C'mon," Evan urges. "Jenna's going to be finished with the downstairs soon. We should probably hurry."

Reluctantly you let go of the doorknob. Half of you wants to reach out and grab it again... but the other half wins out. You blink three times and shake it off.

"Fine," you say, gesturing to the other colorful choices. "Which one next?"

Pick another door (and no, you can't choose the gold door again!)

If you select the *RED* door, *TURN TO PAGE 22*

If you select the *BLUE* door, *TURN TO PAGE 106*

If you select the *GREEN* door, *TURN TO PAGE 136*

If you select the *BLACK* door, *TURN TO PAGE 36*

THE SECRET OF THE AURORA HOTEL

You look up very slowly. Standing in the center of the elevator, between the three of you, is the ghostly presence of a tall, bearded man.

The man from the photograph.

"Alastair!" Jenna cries. "It's him! I mean... it's... it's *you!*"

The ghost turns slowly in her direction, reflecting perfectly in the elevator's mirrored walls. "*Yes,*" he says, nodding politely. The voice you hear seems to come from every direction. It's also vague. Non-corporeal. Almost like it's inside your head.

"Do– Do we have everything?" you ask. Twelve hours ago it would've been impossible to believe you'd be conversing with a ghost. But after everything you've seen tonight, it seems oddly natural. "We should head down to the basement now, right?"

The man who was once Alastair flutters in answer. At one point he almost disappears. When he rematerializes, he stands there smoothing his mustaches. You can tell the movement is more a reflex than a conscious action.

"*No,*" he rasps. "*Up.*"

Evan, quiet until now, finally shifts forward. "Up? Up where?"

"*You must see... my kin.*" At this point the ghost flutters again. His head jerks abruptly over one shoulder, eyes locking on some unseen entity. "*He comes,*" Alastair says hurriedly. "*I cannot be here.*"

"But wait!" Jenna cries. "Kin? Kin who? What's a kin?" Instinctively your cousin reaches for the man's hand, as if to grab his attention or perhaps keep him there. Her fingers pass right through it. "Alastair, we–"

Just as quickly as it appeared, the apparition is gone. You're left standing in the bitter cold, with the sudden urge to get out of the elevator. All three of you are shivering.

"Oh man," Evan says all of a sudden. He's peering down at the manifest. "I can't believe we missed this!" Your cousin points to a name as you and Jenna lean over his shoulder.

"James Roakes," you read aloud. Right next to the name is a room number: 217.

"His *kin!*" Evan cries. "Alastair Roakes's grandson, or great grandson, or great great... whatever. He's here, in the hotel! He's been at the Aurora the whole time!"

The elevator shudders to life as Jenna mashes the 2nd floor button. You notice the electronics on the old elevator are all modern, except for a small, silver-colored keyhole recessed just beneath the new panel.

You go up one level, wait for the doors to open, and peek out into an empty hallway. Less than a minute later you're all standing at the threshold to room 217.

"Now what do we do?" Evan asks. "We can't just go knocking on this guy's door at one o'clock in the–"

Jenna knocks, hard. There's the rattle of a chain latch being undone, and the door opens in a surprisingly short amount of time. Even more surprising is the person who answers.

"Alastair?" your cousins gasp in unison. It reminds you sharply that they're twins.

The man behind the door is tall and bearded, but without the trademark mustache you've seen in the photo. His receding hairline is not nearly as advanced either. Still, he appears as the spitting image of a young Alastair Roakes.

"No," the man says in a velvety voice. "But I suppose I know why you'd think so." He examines each of you in turn, then pokes his head out to scan the empty hall. Finally he steps back and opens the door. "You may as well come in."

You enter the double-sized Roakes suite. It looks far less like a hotel room and much more like a home. Each piece of furniture and decoration looks like it belongs, rather than having been placed there to fill a space or only as an afterthought. The air is steeped in the warmth and aroma of herbal tea.

"Sorry if we woke you," Evan begins. "It's just that–"

"You didn't," James Roakes interrupts. He glides into the kitchen, moving with grace and speed. "Unfortunately for me, I seldom sleep these days. Especially on this night, of all nights."

Jenna's eyes flash brightly. "So you know!" she cries. "About your grandfather, and his ceremony, and All Hallows' Eve!"

"*Great* grandfather," the man corrects her. He pulls forth a mug and pours himself a steaming cup of tea. "And yes. I'm familiar with the story." Mid-sip, he looks over the rim of his cup. "I assume you've seen him as well?"

"Y–Yes," you fumble awkwardly. "We have."

Mr. Roakes nods. "He's here, of course. From time to time he's come to me through the years, usually on this night. I've seen him as reflections, mostly. In mirrors, windows and the like." With the last statement the man motions to a large antique mirror, framed by floral blossoms at each corner.

"Through the years?" Evan notes. "Just how long have you been here?"

Mr. Roakes places his cup carefully back on its saucer. "Nearly all my life," he says. "As have my father, and his father too. Since Alastair's disappearance, there has always been a Roakes at the hotel Aurora." He shrugs. "That's just the way of things."

You're not exactly sure why Alastair told you to visit his great grandson, but you're determined to find out. "What if we could help him?" you ask.

"Help who?"

"Alastair!" Jenna chimes in. You can tell she's doing her best not to sound irritated. "The ceremony he was conducting was never completed. We're guessing that's why he disappeared, and why the nethergate is still open here, at the Aurora."

Mr. Roakes makes a face like he just swallowed a bug. "*Nethergate?*" he asks. "Who told you that?" Evan hands him the photograph and letter in answer. James reads it three times. After the initial shock wears off, he looks back up at you.

"You couldn't repeat the ceremony anyway," he says. "You'd need the artifacts mentioned here. The ones in the photograph, plus–"

One by one, you show him what you've found. James examines the book, the bell, the candle. He cradles the crystal ball skeptically, as if expecting it to suddenly vanish. "What about the fifth artifact?" he asks casually.

Your mouth drops open in shock. "*Fifth* artifact?"

"Yes," James replies. "My grandfather always suspected there was another object involved in whatever his father was trying to do. Something required... or perhaps something that *interfered*." He nods to the four objects scattered across his kitchen table. "One of these items may not be correct," he explains. "And another one might be missing."

Evan and Jenna stare back at you. This isn't what you expected at all!

"Perhaps you should leave well enough alone," James Roakes sighs. "All of this was a long time ago. The Aurora has never truly been at peace, but maybe it's best not to make things worse than they already are."

Jenna tenses up at the words. Now she actually does look irritated. "Why do you think Alastair keeps appearing to you?" she asks James. "What do you think he's trying to accomplish?"

The man sipping his tea looks taken aback by this. "I– I don't know. I supposed I never considered."

"He's coming to you for *help*," Jenna says. "And instead of listening, you're doing your best to ignore him."

The curious expression on Mr. Roakes face only makes things worse. "I don't see how–"

"You *live* here," Jenna continues, "and still you do nothing. This place is your family's legacy, and you don't even look for answers?"

For a moment James Roakes appears stunned. As the seconds tick by however, he quickly recovers. His face goes red with what could be anger. But it could also be shame.

"We're leaving now," Jenna says thankfully, "to go help your great grandfather. Maybe we can. Maybe we can't. But at least we're going to try."

The door closes behind you as the three of you exit the Roakes's Suite. There's the sound of the latch being engaged again, and then silence.

"Wow sis," Evan says. "You were a bulldog! I've never seen you like that before."

Jenna's expression fades back into a smile. It looks a lot better than way. "Sorry," she apologizes. "After all the stuff we've been through tonight, I guess I'm on edge."

"No," you cut in. "You were absolutely right. We're trying our best to help, and that guy's trying to... well, *not* help."

Your cousin laughs as she pops another piece of gum in her mouth. "*Not* help?" she snorts. "Is that the technical term for it?"

"Yeah," you elbow her. "It is."

Evan is staring down at the manifest again. "This is the top level of the hotel," he says. "If James Roakes is right, and we do need another artifact, there are still a few rooms we could check out."

"But we don't even know what we're looking for," you point out.

Your cousin shrugs. "True. But maybe we'll know it when we see it."

The three of you look up and down both sides of the empty hallway.

"Alright cuz," Jenna says. "We've been dragging you around this place all night long–"

"Morning, technically," Evan corrects her.

Jenna frowns at him before turning back to you. "Why don't you take the lead here and decide where we're going next?"

To check out room 202, *HEAD OVER TO PAGE 140*

If room 205 sounds luckier to you, *TURN TO PAGE 89*

Or maybe you like the sound of room 212? If so, *GO TO PAGE 24*

150

You crunch your way to the dead center of the roof, where the cupola presides over everything. It's a white, eight-sided structure made up almost entirely of glass panes. Centered at its peak, past a small dome, are the frozen remnants of what might've been a flag.

"Get in!" Jenna shouts. She's shivering, even with both arms wrapped around herself. "Hurry!"

The inside of the cupola looks calm and inviting. Evan circles around it until he finds a series of glass panes framed by a door. He tries it... but it's locked. You notice a small keyhole beneath the knob.

"Break one of the panes if we have to," Jenna orders. She points down to the distant ground. "You won't even be able to tell from down there."

Evan shakes his head. Evidently he hates the whole idea. "Maybe we should just skip–"

"No!" Jenna shouts. "We have to be thorough! Besides, I'm freezing!" She looks to you pleadingly. "Come on Scotty, just do it! Here, this pane is already cracked anyway. Dad will never know."

Reluctantly you step over to the cracked pane of glass. You ball your hand into a fist... pull it back...

"Hang on!" Evan cries, stopping you mid-swing. He wriggles out of his sweatshirt and wraps it three times around your arm. It's not ideal, but at least it offers some protection. "Okay," he tells you. "Now try it."

Wait! Do you happen to have the cupola key? If so, what shape is its handle? Add up all the letters of that word using the chart below, then *GO TO THAT PAGE*

A = 1	F = 6	K = 11	P = 16	U = 21	Z = 26
B = 2	G = 7	L = 12	Q = 17	V = 22	Example:
C = 3	H = 8	M = 13	R = 18	W = 23	ANNA =
D = 4	I = 9	N = 14	S = 19	X = 24	1+14+14+1
E = 5	J = 10	O = 15	T = 20	Y = 25	= 30

If you don't have the cupola key, you'll just have to wing it. Punch through the glass by flipping two coins:

If both coins come up *HEADS* when you flip them, *GO TO PAGE 57*

If either or both coins show *TAILS* after the toss, *HEAD TO PAGE 121*

152

You pick up a ghost fork and a ghost knife. No one at the table even acknowledges you. Finally, without ceremony, you tear into the roast beef.

You chew slowly, expecting something to happen. Nothing does. The meat is excellent actually. You find it tender, tasty, and pink in the center.

Bite after bite you keep eating, compelled by a strange, ravenous hunger. It's almost as if you hadn't already downed an entire cheeseburger just a few hours earlier. Jenna watches you, thoroughly impressed. Even some of the other ghosts look on in admiration.

You continue eating until you feel Jenna's hand on your arm. "Scotty," your cousin whispers, "we should go. There's something... I don't know, there's something weird about this."

You laugh loudly as you stab another piece of meat. "Weird? We're guests at a ghost banquet in a century-old dining hall just after midnight, in the wee hours of Halloween. What could possibly be weird?"

"I mean, well, I was thinking we should–"

"Are you gonna eat that?" you ask, pointing. Rather than wait for an answer you slide your cousin's plate over in front you.

"No, but–"

"Good. Thanks." Your stomach rumbles, causing you to wonder if there will be seconds. Maybe you should look around for the serving ghost...

"Cuz, let's go!" Jenna says. Now she's actually pulling you. Gently at first, and then with a lot more effort.

"Do you think there will be dessert?"

"We have to *leave!*" Jenna cries. Her voice is so loud she's practically shouting. "NOW!"

A fog seems to lift from your head. Clarity descends as you allow Jenna to pull you out of your chair and away from the table. One of the ghosts glances up with an expression of indignity. "I– I'm okay now," you tell your cousin. "Thanks."

Jenna lets loose a tremendous sigh of relief. "Good," she says, pushing you through a large wooden archway. "Now let's get out of here. For a minute there I thought you were going to eat the tablecloth too!"

Better go while you still can.

Make your way into the hotel lounge *BY TURNING TO PAGE 49*

Or investigate the Aurora's kitchen when you *GO TO PAGE 117*

You enter a room filled with heavy oaken furniture and crisp white linens. The floor is oak and the walls as well; you feel as if you've walked through the threshold and into a mountain lodge.

"What's with this room?" you ask.

"Not sure," Evan says. "But dad likes it, so he left it as is."

You begin your search for the artifacts in the photo. There are no candles, no books, no bell or crystal ball. The drawers are large and empty, the floors polished and smooth. Everything in here is neat and clean and easy to check.

"Looks empty," you say. "I guess we should–"

Suddenly you feel a presence. A *pressure.* It shoves you downward, forcing you to your knees. You look over at Evan and he's feeling it too. Your cousin crumples into a push-up position. His arms give out and he's face down on the floor.

"What is it?" he grunts. You can tell he's having a hard time breathing.

"I don't know!" You try to stand but there's just no way. There's a hum in the air now, too. A vibration that seems to get louder and more pronounced as the pressure increases. Soon you're also hugging the floor. Struggling to push up against it...

A voice floats into your head, from somewhere off to the left. There's nothing in that direction, you realize. Just a dresser and its mirror.

"*Don't fight it!*" the voice tells you. "*It only makes it worse...*"

The voice is deep, resonant, authoritative. You can't tell if it's stern and fatherly, or cold and sinister...

Do you fight back against the unknown force? If so, *FLIP BACK TO PAGE 13*
Or maybe you should listen to the ghost voice? To not fight back, *GO TO PAGE 129*

154

The vase is large... large enough to hide something. You step forward to check it out.

"That thing doesn't have any hands," Evan points out.

"True," you say, "but maybe at one point it did." You run your fingers over the painted black surface, feeling the brush strokes beneath. "Whatever it *did* have, someone covered it up."

The vase is as long as your arm. The inside is darkness. You consider upending it, to see what's inside. Then again, the contents could be fragile...

If you upend the vase, *TURN TO PAGE 130*
If you reach inside the vase, *GO TO PAGE 73*

After several moments of silence you grab Jenna by the wrist and pull her to her feet. The kitchen appears empty. For now.

"Back," you tell her. "The way we came."

Quickly but carefully you hustle your way through the steamy kitchen. Somehow you avoid running into anyone else, or burning yourself on the searing hot maze of boiling pots and kettles.

"The kitchen was a bad idea," Jenna admits. "But come this way. I have a better place for us to check..."

Follow Jenna into a much better scenario when you *TURN TO PAGE 49*

156

Slogging back across the frozen roof is even colder the second time around. You claw your way down the icy fire escape and stumble through the door to the stairwell Evan mentioned. Your luck continues as you find it unlocked.

In the second floor hallway Jenna stops and puts her hands on her knees. "Can we just rest here for a minute?" she begs. Melting snow drips from the tip of her nose. "Or maybe go to the lobby and stand in front of the fireplace for a little while?"

You lay a reassuring hand on your cousin's shoulder. "Not yet," you say. "We're almost done. We have to do this for you dad. And for Alastair."

Jenna nods. Smiles. Her tongue snakes out as she blows another pink bubble. This time you do reach out and pop it. She laughs. "Alright cuz. Let's go."

Head back to the elevator *OVER ON PAGE 137*

You sneak back through the main lobby and past the Grand Staircase. Agnes is back at the front desk, but you stay far enough away that she doesn't even notice you. Eventually you arrive at the hotel's main elevator.

"Why didn't we take this thing before?" you ask your cousin.

Jenna shrugs. "Because the other ways were more fun?" You follow her inside. Although the elevator itself is old, the instrument panel consists of newly-added electronics. All except for an odd, silver-looking keyhole recessed just beneath the new panel.

"Hit it," Jenna tells you.

You thumb the thick plastic '1' button. It lights right up, and the doors open with a universal *ding.*

One floor later the doors open again and you're staring at your cousin Evan. He looks totally frazzled but overwhelmingly relieved to see you.

"Did you get anything?" he asks quickly. You motion him into the elevator so the three of you don't have to talk out in the hallway.

"Only this," Jenna smirks, holding up the book. Less theatrically she shows him the candle. "Oh, and *this* too."

Evan lets loose a huge sigh of relief. "That's great!" Without saying another word he holds up two objects: a crystal ball and a small silver bell, both identical to the ones in Alastair's photograph.

"You did good bro!" Jenna cries. She hugs him, and for one brief scary moment he almost drops the ball. Gingerly you take it away from him.

"So that's everything?" you ask. "All four artifacts and we're ready to go?"

The elevator is suddenly ripped by a blast of arctic cold. The skin on your arms prickles. The hairs stand up on the back of your neck.

"*Not exactly...*" rasps a voice that doesn't belong to any of you.

Whoa, what's going on? Better find out fast by *HEADING TO PAGE 146*

158

Your arms are shaking. Or maybe it's Jenna. Or the ladder. Or all three.

"I think it's that far one," you tell your cousin. "The one with the really weird symbol."

Jenna shifts. Reaches out for it. But she leans too far to one side, and a spark of terror shoots through you as you realize you're going to fall. Your cousin screams.

"Scotty!"

You feel your center of gravity move past the point of no return. The ladder tips out from beneath you, and you both go tumbling to the ground. The fall seems endless. You throw your arms out, but your body twists and one elbow gets caught behind your back... just as the full weight of your cousin lands directly on top of you.

Snap.

Jenna gets away with a few scrapes and bruises, but the agony of your broken arm is nothing compared to the shame of your Uncle's grave disappointment. You lower your head all the way to the hospital, wondering how you'll ever explain this to your parents.

For now, at least, your adventure has come to

THE END

"Be right back!" you tell Evan. Then, before your cousin can protest, you hang from the ledge and drop into the warm, dry air.

The sand is a lot softer than it first looked. You sink in up to your knees, then tumble backward down the slope of the dune itself. Finally you reach solid ground and approach the white object you saw earlier. Long and cylindrical, you pull it free from the sands... and recognize it in an instant.

A bone!

Panic grips you as you toss the bone away. You can't see anything else from here. Sand is getting everywhere now. It's in your shoes, under your shirt – everywhere it touches it clings to your skin. You scratch the back of your neck uncomfortably, deciding you've definitely had enough of this place.

"Evan, I'm coming up!" you shout. "See if you can throw down a bed sheet or–"

Your stomach drops out from under you as you turn around. Evan's gone! In fact, *everything* is gone – even the Aurora!

Slowly you spin around. As impossible as it seems, there's nothing in any direction but sand, dirt, and dunes. The sun beats down on you from above, seeming a lot hotter than before.

You don't have a map, or a direction, or even a clue as to where you are. You don't even have a water bottle.

All you have left is the taste of fear in your mouth, as you realize this is certainly

THE END

160

"You do the bathroom," you tell Evan. "I got this."

A minute later you've searched the drawers, the walls, even the egg chair that dominates one corner of the room. You sit down in it to get a sense of the room... or maybe because you've never sat in an egg chair before and always wanted to.

"Anything yet?" your cousin calls from the bathroom.

"Nope."

The last thing you do is check under the bed. It's blocked by a mass of gears and gadgets. You follow a series of wires to the coin-operated machine on one side, then fish into your pocket and pull out a quarter.

When Evan emerges from the bathroom you're flat on your back, lying on the bed while it spins in dizzying circles. The disco ball glimmers above you.

"Quit foolin' around," Evan tells you. "We've got other rooms to check."

Room 119 is next on the list. Check it out *OVER ON PAGE 69*

SNEAK PEEK

Welcome to the Heidelberg Physics Laboratory!

You are JEREMY HELLER, a recent graduate from the prestigious University of Zurich, where you received a Masters Degree in particle physics. You've got your first real job working at the Heidelberg Physics Laboratory, high in the Swiss Alps. Everyone from your university applied for the position, but you were the only one to be accepted. You can't believe how lucky you are!

You've only been working there a week, but already the laboratory is full of excitement. Built deep within the mountain is a particle accelerator, a long oval-shaped track that shoots atoms around and around really fast. The atoms are smashed into other atoms close to the speed of light, and the laboratory measures the pieces that come out. Cool!

Today is an especially important day. After months of testing, the physicists at the laboratory are smashing atoms together in a way that they hope will reveal a new subatomic particle: the Causality Neutrino. It would be the greatest physics discovery in the past century. And you might be a part of it!

You're all ready to get to work. You're wearing your white lab coat over dress clothes, and are riding the gondola all the way to the top of the mountain. From there you will need to take an elevator deep underground. Building the laboratory deep within the mountain ensures that the equipment is shielded by thousands of meters of rock, in case anything goes wrong. Although that seems highly unlikely–the physicists there are the best in the world!

You step off the gondola onto the mountain peak. The wind whips your lab coat all around, and the air feels like a thousand tiny needles on your face. Better get inside!

162

You hear the distant sound of machinery slowly grinding to life. The elevator is beginning to make its journey all the way to the surface. The wind is especially chilling this day, and already you can feel your curly black hair freezing to your head. Instead of wearing your nicest clothes for the demonstration, maybe you should have dressed warmer!

There's a muted *ding* as the elevator car arrives. The doors open slowly, and you jump through before they've barely opened. You press your shoulder against the wall of the car, trying to stay as far from the door as possible.

There are only two buttons: 'S' for Surface, and 'L' for Laboratory. You punch the 'L' with frozen fingers and the button glows yellow.

"Hey, wait!" drifts a voice from outside.

Did you imagine it? You lean your head sideways to take a look. The gondola station is a hundred feet away, and a new car has just come to a stop, rocking slightly on its cable. The door opens and a stream of people come pouring out, huddled in dark clothes.

One of them waves. "Hold the elevator!" It sounds like a girl.

Suffering the cold, you obediently stick your hand out to keep the doors from closing.

The people come jogging up the path and into the elevator. The person who waved is a girl, about your age, bundled head to toe in thick clothes. Straight blonde hair sticks out from underneath a woven cap and runs down her back.

"Thank you!" she says, out of breath. Her cheeks are flushed from the cold. "It would have been miserable waiting for the elevator car to go down and up again. I wish they'd build a waiting area shielded from the cold!"

You frown. She doesn't look like she works at the laboratory. "What are you doing here?" you blurt out.

The girl laughs. "That's not very polite." You begin to apologize, but she holds up a hand and says, "I'm teasing, I'm teasing. I'm here today for the demonstration. My father is Doctor Kessler."

You stare at the girl, awestruck. "Your father is Doctor Kessler?"

She gives a big nod. "Uh huh. So you'd better be nice to me, or I can get you in trouble."

You lick your lips out of nervousness. Kessler is the head physicist at the laboratory, in charge of the entire particle accelerator! If he finds out you were rude to his daughter...

The girl lets out a stream of giggles. "I'm just teasing you again. I wouldn't get you in trouble. You lab guys are easy to fluster." She sticks out a gloved hand. "Nice to meet you, Heller. I'm Penny. Penny Kessler."

Her glove is cold as you shake it. "How'd you know my name?"

Her face grows serious. "Dad was complaining last night about one of the interns. I assumed it was you. Looks like I was right, huh?"

Your mouth hangs open, horrified.

Penny's face is suddenly split by a wicked grin. "Okay, you've got me again. My dad's never mentioned you. I knew your name because it's on your name tag, silly." She points.

You look down at your coat breast, where a plastic clip-on tag says: J. HELLER. "Are you always this cruel to people you've just met?" you ask.

She flashes a white smile. "Just being friendly! Hey—no more joking around." She points to the path, where the other four men from the gondola are approaching the elevator. "Those are investors from the city. They're here to see the demo. If it doesn't go well, dad says they're going to pull their funding."

Uh oh. You had heard rumors that the investors weren't happy, but had assumed they weren't true.

The four men pile into the elevator. They're each wearing dark coats which drape to their ankles, with full suits underneath. One of them frowns at you. "Vat are ve vaiting for" he asks in a German accent.

You realize your hand is still holding the car. "Oh, sorry," you say, removing it. The man nods to himself.

The doors close.

164

The elevator makes its slow descent into the mountain. As you do every time, you wonder how a single elevator could travel so far. The laboratory must be at least a kilometer underground. Your ears pop, so you move your jaw around to unclog your ears, like you're on an airplane. About a minute later you have to do it again.

Finally the hum of the elevator reaches a lower pitch as you slow down, and then stop completely.

The doors open.

The entrance room to the Heidelberg Physics Laboratory feels like the lair of a James Bond villain: the side walls are carved rock, making it obvious you are deep inside a mountain, and the air has a cool, drafty feel. The wall directly opposite you has a single, massive door in the center. It's five meters tall and three wide, and covered with blinking lights and electronics. It's made of dull metal, and you know it can withstand a nuclear explosion, if need be.

The room is empty except for a man standing next to the big door with his hands folded in front of him. He's wearing a lab coat just like yours. "Welcome to the Heidelberg Laboratory!" he says to the investors. "I'm Doctor Kessler."

The men walk forward and shake his hand formally. Kessler doesn't even seem to notice his daughter.

"In order to access the laboratory," Kessler tells the investors, "you must pass through our Decontamination Chamber. It is perfectly harmless, I assure you: just a little bit of steam and a computer scan, and you will be through to the other side."

He turns and punches a code into a keypad on the wall. You hear the sound of three massive bolts retracting, and the blast door slowly swings open. "There's room for all of you, come on now." He ushers the four men inside with a nervous laugh, then enters himself, closing the door behind him.

Penny crosses her arms over her chest. "Nice to see you too, father."

"I'm sure he's just nervous because of the investors," you say.

"Yeah, I'm sure that's it," Penny says. She doesn't sound like she believes you.

You go to the door to the Decontamination Chamber, where there's a computer screen on the wall. You can see the five men inside being blasted with jets of air. "It will only take a minute," you call over your shoulder. "Then we can go."

You realize Penny is looking at the map on the wall. You walk over to her. "Wow, this place is big," she says.

"It sure is," you say. You hear a computerized beep across the room. "Come on, it's our turn."

The door opens into a long, cylindrical room, with walls that curve upward toward the ceiling. It reminds you of a coke can on its side. There's a metallic echo as you step inside.

"Stand away from the door," you instruct. Penny obeys, and watches as the door closes behind you with a loud KONG.

"Hold your hands out to the side," you say while typing your credentials into the computer on the wall. "It won't hurt, I promise."

"Yessir, mister physicist, sir."

You frown. "Are you making fun of me?"

She bats her eyelashes. "Of course not."

You finish entering the protocol into the computer, and there's a loud whine like a jet engine spinning up. Jets in the floor and walls blast you with scalding air, fluttering your lab coat around like you're in a tornado. While that's occurring, a door opens in the ceiling and a device like a laser pointer sticks out. A single green laser beam shoots out of the end in your direction, then spreads out into a long fan-shaped beam. The beam moves up and down, scanning first your body, then Penny's.

The laser disappears back into the ceiling, and then the jets cease as quickly as they had begun.

You glance over at Penny and see that she's still gritting her teeth and squeezing her eyes shut. "All done, Miss Kessler," you say with exaggerated politeness. "There's no need to be afraid, now."

She opens one eye, looks around the room, then opens the other. She puts her arms down. "Do you enjoy scaring all the visitors, Jeremy?"

"Just the ones who tease me first."

She gives you a big grin. "I think I'm going to like you, Jeremy."

You turn away to conceal your own embarrassed smile, and press the button at the other end of the decontamination room. The far door opens with a hiss of air and pressure release.

You gesture to the room. "Penny, welcome to the Heidelberg Laboratory."

166

The main Control Room of the laboratory is busier than usual. A dozen of the Senior Physicists scurry from one computer station to another, checking instrument readings and making notes on their clipboards. The entire far wall is covered in glass, giving a view into a tube-like room beyond. The rest of the walls are filled with computer screens showing various graphs of data and video feeds of the facility.

"What's that?" Penny points to the glass wall.

"That's a section of the particle accelerator," you explain. "It's like a giant oval track, over five kilometers long. See those ridges inside? With the coils? Those are powerful electromagnets, which are used to speed up the particles faster and faster."

"Ohh, cool," Penny says.

You lead her over to a corner of the room, where a single computer screen sits at a lonely computer desk. "This is where I work."

She blinks. "This is all you do?"

"Hey, I'm just an intern. I'm new. It may not look like much, but I still have an important job."

"Which is?"

"I'm in charge of monitoring the power levels for the facility," you say. "The particle accelerator has its own nuclear reactor. It was on the map, if you saw it. When we're performing our tests, the accelerator draws a lot of power. My job is to monitor this power level, make sure it's not drawing too much, and to notify anyone if the drain gets too high."

Penny raises an eyebrow. "That's it?"

"Hey, it's important," you say weakly.

"Heller!" someone yells across the room. It's your boss, Doctor Almer. He comes storming over. "Heller, what are you doing?"

"I'm just showing Penny around."

He swings his eyes toward her. "Who?"

"This is Doctor Kessler's daughter."

"Ohh." His entire demeanor changes. "Miss Kessler! Your father is wonderful to work with. Simply wonderful. You should be in the observation lounge with the other visitors."

He glances at you, as if it's your fault.

Penny makes a face. "Can't I stay here with Jeremy? I don't want to be stuck with all those investors..."

Almer is dragging her away. Penny looks back at you pleadingly.

What will *you* do, when you're forced to deal with

THE STRANGE PHYSICS
OF THE
HEIDELBERG LABORATORY

ABOUT THE AUTHORS

Danny McAleese started writing fantasy fiction during the golden age of Dungeons & Dragons, way back in the heady, adventure-filled days of the 1980's. His short stories, The Exit, and Momentum, made him the Grand Prize winner of Blizzard Entertainment's 2011 Global Fiction Writing contest.

He currently lives in NY, along with his wife, four children, three dogs, and a whole lot of chaos. www.dannymcaleese.com

David Kristoph lives in Virginia with his wonderful wife and two not-quite German Shepherds. He's a fantastic reader, great videogamer, good chess player, average cyclist, and mediocre runner. He's also a member of the Planetary Society, patron of StarTalk Radio, amateur astronomer and general space enthusiast. He writes mostly Science Fiction and Fantasy. www.DavidKristoph.com

THE SECRET OF THE AURORA HOTEL

Printed in Great Britain
by Amazon